D1604216

THE Life and Death of JOHNNY RINGO

Center Point
Large Print

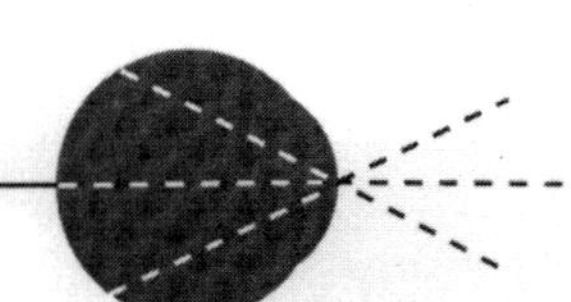

This Large Print Book carries the Seal of Approval of N.A.V.H.

ॐ श्री गणेशाय नमः

RAY HOGAN

THE *Life and Death of* JOHNNY RINGO

CENTER POINT PUBLISHING
THORNDIKE, MAINE

TO MIKE and JUDEE
in Phoenix, Arizona

This Center Point Large Print edition
is published in the year 2003 by arrangement with
Golden West Literary Agency.

The text of this Large Print edition is unabridged. In other aspects, this book may vary from the original edition. Printed in Thailand. Set in 16-point Times New Roman type by Bill Coskrey and Gary Socquet.

ISBN 1-58547-245-X

Cataloging-in-Publication data is available from the Library of Congress.

FOREWORD

The story of tall, inscrutable John Ringo is thoroughly intertwined with the chronicle of Arizona's tumultuous Tombstone. Together they rose to fame, scrawled their legends across the pages of history with blood, and died. But unlike the lusty town that sprang to life on Goose Flats as the result of one man's dream, John Ringo came riding across the blue-shadowed hills into destiny, seemingly out of nowhere.

Diligent search has failed to turn up his actual birth date, his parentage, or his homeland. He was a close-mouthed man and what few records existed that might have shed some light on his early background were lost in the fire that destroyed the Mason County, Texas, courthouse in 1877. As a result of this lack of factual information, a vast amount of guesswork and speculation has arisen.

Some believe he was born in Missouri. Others say Texas, or California, even Maryland. Most think his real name was Ringgold, that he shortened it to Ringo to protect his family from his odorous reputation. It is said he rode with Quantrill and his band of ruthless desperadoes; that he was kin to those notorious outlaws, the Younger brothers; that he was college-educated, scion of a prominent, wealthy family fallen from high estate; that he was a most chivalrous gentleman of unquestioned loyalty, honesty, and courage.

The limited results of extensive investigation bear out only a small part of those conclusions. My own considerations lead me to believe he was born in Texas, probably around 1844. His name likely was Ringo in the beginning; no man named Ringgold, wishing to conceal his identity, would choose another so similar, so alike in sound.

All agree he had a good education for his time (probably an eighth-grade fulfillment, or possibly one of high-school level). Records of Quantrill's band list no John Ringo (or Ringgold) on the rosters. And I could find no connection with the Youngers (particularly any which proved he had a grandfather by that name in California; quite to the contrary, in fact). That he was a brave man possessed of a violent heart and fiercely burning loyalties, a soft-spoken gentleman strangely out of a gentleman's element, is indisputable.

Evidence eventually may come to light that will solve the mystery of John Ringo, but until such proof is presented there is little that can be relied upon except, of course, his years in Tombstone.

This story of John Ringo, therefore, is based on the facts that are available and is narrated in fictional form to make its presentation more appealing. It has been a matter of clothing a skeleton with flesh, placing muscle and skin on the stark bones of scattered truths. It could have been the way he lived and died. This could have been the way it happened—the life and death of Johnny Ringo. . . .

—Ray Hogan

PROLOGUE

He was sitting upright beneath a twisted, sun-scorched oak tree. There was a neat hole in his right temple, a ragged, bloody area on the top of his head where the bullet had emerged. A portion of his scalp was missing, as though a knife-wielding Apache, still carrying vengeance in his heart for the loss of his Arizona homeland, might have taken a hand in the grisly affair.

John Yoast knelt down for a closer look. There was something familiar about the dead man. He stiffened, drew back suddenly.

"My God—it's Johnny Ringo!"

1

"I've had enough of Texas," Ringo said in that dry, aloof way of his. "And I think Texas has had enough of me."

Olney looked up from his drink. They were the only patrons in the squat, thick-walled little saloon. "Same here. But you ain't got a lawman doggin' your trail like I have."

"Had my share," Ringo drawled. "And I'm tired of it. Think I'd like to try ranching for a spell. Maybe punch cows for somebody and then, later on, get a place of my own."

Olney snorted. "You'd never stick with it. After packin' a gun long as you have, and that Hoodoo War thing over in Mason County you and Scott Cooley got mixed up in, be too damn tame to suit you."

"Maybe not," Ringo said, glancing down at the ivory-handled forty-fives on his hips. A ruggedly handsome man, he had strong, usually somber features, dark-auburn hair, and ice-blue eyes. He spoke in a careful, cultured manner that reflected a background of education and breeding.

"Somethin' else," Olney said. "They'd never leave you be. Always be somebody lookin' to build a reputation, proddin' you, tryin' to push you into a fight."

"Nothing new there. Man learns the hard way to look after himself. He gets good at it, then the rest follows naturally. It will happen whether I stay here in Texas, go back to Wichita, or move on to the territories."

Olney wagged his head. "Well, I ain't sayin' it's a bum idea. I'm only tellin' you how it will prob'ly work out."

Ringo poured himself another drink from the near-empty bottle. He glanced at the bartender, motioned for a fresh supply of the fiery liquor. In silence Olney watched him tip the glass to his long lips and drink. The tall, sardonic Ringo's capacity for whiskey was awesome. They had been in the saloon less than three hours and were almost through the second quart, only a small part of which Joe Olney had drunk.

"You play the cards you've been dealt," Ringo murmured, his brooding face tipped downward. "Sometimes they're good, sometimes bad. Had no choice in Mason County."

"Sure, sure," Olney agreed. "Ain't sayin' you did. I just meant—"

"Man has to stand by his friends, regardless."

"Meaning Scott Cooley?"

"Mostly. There were others. Cooley was the one who brought me into it."

Olney helped himself to the new bottle. Two riders loped down the empty street that fronted the saloon. Both Ringo and Olney swung their attention to them, watched with close, narrow interest through the dusty window glass. The horsemen rode on.

Olney said, "Never did get the straight of that Hoodoo War business. Trouble between the Dutchmen and the Americans, wasn't it?"

Ringo nodded. "Always was bad blood between them, with the law generally siding the Dutchmen all the way."

"Reckon what got Cooley all het up about it was that deputy—what was his name—Wohrle—killin' off his pa."

"He wasn't Cooley's real father," Ringo said. "Tim Williamson, his name was. He and his wife had taken Scott in as a boy, raised him like their own. One day Wohrle came out to the ranch where Tim worked and arrested him on some trumped-up charge that didn't amount to anything. Insisted on him riding back to the courthouse in Mason. On the way, twelve men, all with their faces blacked up, jumped them. They shot Tim down and Wohrle made no move to stop them. Was plain murder."

"Then Cooley killed Wohrle," Olney finished.

Ringo shifted his lean body. "Made a good job of it. Shot the deputy six times, stabbed him, and took his scalp."

"He was a wild one," Olney said, clucking softly. "Recollect seein' him once. Looked dark, like he was part Indian."

"Maybe he was, I don't know. But he sure had a big hate on for them, even worse than he did for Pete Bader and the rest of the men in that ambush."

"He get them, too?"

"Most of them. He sent word out to all of us right after he killed the deputy and we joined up at George Gladden's place at Cold Springs. There were Mose and John Beard, along with a half a dozen others who had been working around in that part of the country. Scott said he was out to even things with the Dutchmen and the law and asked us to throw in with him. We'd all had a taste of trouble from both, so we did.

"Before we could get started doing anything, John Clark, the sheriff at Mason, and Wohrle's boss, decided to stop us. Guess he figured things were brewing. Clark didn't have much guts so he figured another ambush like they pulled on Tim was the safest way to handle it. He sent John Cheney out to Cold Springs with word that some people in town wanted to see Gladden and Mose Beard."

"Cheney," Olney said and spat. "Lousy tinhorn gambler!"

"We figured he was on the square, though, and so did Mose and George. They followed him in to Mason but when they got near Keller's Store, sixty men rode down on them. Sixty men to their two."

"That sheriff sure wasn't takin' no chances!" Joe Olney said, cocking his head to one side. "Why'nt he just call out the whole Texas Rangers?"

"Later they did," Ringo said with a half smile. "Anyway, Gladden caught a bullet first off but it didn't finish him. Mose hit the ground dead. Then to make matters worse,

Pete Bader, one of the twelve who had killed Williamson, saw a gold ring on Mose's finger he fancied. He didn't bother to pull it off—just pulled his knife and whacked off the finger to get to it.

"That put things to rolling good. Soon as Gladden was healed up and John Beard had returned from burying his brother, Scott took the bunch into town to have it out with Clark. Another one of the boys, Bill Williams, and I went after Cheney. We found him at his place on Comanche Creek and put a few bullets into his lying skin. Then we went on to Mason where Scott and the others were."

"You get Clark?"

"Never did. He'd holed up. We stayed around several days looking for him but failed. Was one little fracas between the Dutchmen and us but we finally gave it up and rode on. Clark then resigned and left the country—just dropped out of sight. Cooley was pretty hot about it but he started then after Bader and the rest."

"Where were the Rangers while all this was goin' on?"

Ringo stared at a fly-specked calendar on the wall opposite, eyes half closed, face dark. He lifted his glass, took another long swallow.

"They were supposed to be hunting us. Jones had quite a crew working the hills but Cooley had once been a Ranger and he had a lot of friends in the ranks. Besides, it looked to most like the law in Mason County was taking sides with the Germans; so a lot of them didn't work very hard at the search. Fact is, a dozen or so resigned when Jones put the bee on them to find Cooley and the rest of us, or quit.

"Scott and I finally located Bader—or thought we did.

We heard he was on a place over near Llano. We got the wrong ranch and it was Pete's brother, Charley, we cut down."

"That when Marshal Strickland caught up with you and Cooley and threw the both of you in the jug?"

"Not long after. He locked us up in Burnet but a lot of people didn't like the idea, so he moved us to Austin. Same thing happened there. He moved us again, this time to the Lampasas County jail. Weren't there long, either. About three dozen citizens showed up and sprung us. We rode off into the hills, and holed up. While we were in jail Gladden and John Beard found Pete Bader and killed him."

"That end it?"

"No. Scott still wanted to clean up the rest of the twelve who had murdered Tim. Soon as the outfit was together again, we started in. But most of the men Cooley wanted had disappeared. Couple had died, rest just weren't around any more. Things sort of slowed down and there wasn't much doing. Some of the boys drifted away.

"One day Cooley himself rode off and had one of his spells and died. That broke up the bunch for sure and Gladden and I decided we'd best take a run up to Kansas and have a look around. The Rangers had a real drive going on and it wasn't exactly healthy around Mason.

"Before we could pull out we got ourselves trapped at Moseley's Ranch and were accused of Pete Bader's murder. They turned me loose after the hearing—I was in jail at Austin at the time Pete was killed—but they sentenced George to ninety-nine years in the pen. He's still there."

Ringo paused. He twirled the glass tumbler between his

long fingers, studied the sloshing amber liquor in the container moodily. "Often wonder why I didn't get mine during all that shooting. Had some close calls but somehow I always came through."

"Bullet somewhere for every man who lives by a gun," Olney said firmly. "One thing I've always believed. Reckon yours wasn't one of them."

"Wouldn't particularly matter to me," Ringo said indifferently. "Sometimes I think it might have been better. Man gets in over his head mighty fast. Then it takes a long time to climb back out—and generally he never makes it."

"That's for certain," Olney agreed morosely. "Reckon if I had things to do over again, I'd do different. But they ain't no use talkin' about that now. What's done is done. If you're ridin' on, I'll trail along with you—you bein' willin'. Any special place you're heading?"

"Man by the name of Hill once offered me a job on his ranch. Place up on the New Mexico-Arizona line—the San Simon Valley country. Thought I'd take him up on his proposition."

"Carrying a gun or punchin' cattle?"

"Punching cattle," Ringo said, rising. He stood by the table, stretched his muscular, six-foot-two-inch body. He glanced out into the empty street. "Can't see much sense in hanging around here any longer. I'm ready to ride if you are."

"I'm ready," Olney said promptly. "Fact is, I've been ready ever since that sheriff at Burnet got on my tail."

Ringo gave him a half smile, reached for the near-empty bottle of whiskey. He palmed the cork into its neck sharply, tucked it under his arm.

"Expect we'd better take this along," he said, dropping a scatter of coins onto the table. "Might be a long ride to the next saloon."

2

Joe Olney had been partly right.

Hill had stood behind his offer of a job and he was a good boss, but cowpunching was a hard, grinding existence with no stimulation and few rewards. Within a year's time John Ringo found himself weary of it all. But he hung on. Every day that dragged by pushed the past farther into the background. Eventually he would become a forgotten man—and with that the recollection of his deeds would fade.

Then he could move about over the land as he pleased, without fear or reservation. He could even go home again, see if any of his family still lived. Perhaps his dreams of a wife and a ranch of his own might then come true; a man wouldn't mind the grueling labor so much if he worked for himself.

And so he stayed with it. Then, late one summer afternoon in 1879 he returned to the ranch house, bored in spirit, worn physically. He had spent most of the day hazing a small jag of steers from a lower corner of Hill's range to a better graze some miles to the west. The stubborn brutes had resisted him at every opportunity and by the time the chore was done, he was utterly exhausted.

When he rode into the yard and pulled up at the hitch rack, he saw half a dozen strange horses in the corral. Dismounting, he stood for a time studying them. One, a huge black with a single white stocking, looked familiar. A shout from the house brought him around.

"Ringo! You old son of a gun! Never figured to see you wet-nursing cows!"

Ringo stared, then started forward quickly, hand outstretched. "Curly Bill Brocius! Haven't seen you since that night in Dodge City. What are you doing here?"

Brocius, a giant of a man with a broad grin, black curly hair and mustache, stepped off the gallery that fronted Hill's house. Legs spraddled, hands on hips, eyes laughing, he was the same Curly Bill that Ringo had ridden with on a dozen flaming exploits in Kansas and other places.

Brocius winked. "Little business over Lordsburg way," he said, taking Ringo's hand. "But some of the good citizens decided they didn't exactly like the way we done things—so we figured we'd better move on."

Ringo smiled. "Cattle business?"

Curly Bill shook his great head. "Stagecoach business, pardner! Don't fool much with cattle no more. Ain't worth it when there's a lot of easy money just floating around."

"Where you hanging out? Someplace close by?"

"Nope, a burg called Tombstone—town that sprung up over in Arizona territory. And another dump called Charleston, just south of it. It's close to Old Man Clanton's ranch in the San Pedro Valley. We use 'em all."

"Clanton? Do I know him?"

"Doubt it. He's an old mossy-horn Texan. Got three boys, all ornery as he is. He sort of heads up the bunch. You looking for a place to light?"

"Not especially," Ringo replied. "Got a job here with Hill—but I'm damn sick of punching cows."

Brocius considered the tall rider thoughtfully. Then, "Sure ain't no job for the likes of you," he said. "And we can always use a fast gun. You interested?"

John Ringo stared out across the choppy hills. Curly Bill's words stirred him, reawakened the old need for thrill, for excitement, he had so determinedly ignored. But if he gave in now, if he turned again to the gun . . .

"What do you say, Johnny?"

This was where the river forked. He had his choice. He could go on just as he was, grubbing out a hard living, hoping for a future that was problematical at best—or he could go back to the good times, the big money, the wild, carefree, dangerous way of life. It was up to him.

"Why not?" Ringo said suddenly, a smile breaking across his lips. "Man lives but one time. Might as well enjoy every minute of it."

"Good!" Brocius exclaimed, slapping him on the back. "Come on inside and meet some of the boys. Rest you'll see when we get back to Charleston."

Ringo followed Brocius into the house. Hill and the visitors had gathered in the kitchen. They were sitting around a table, a quart bottle of whiskey in front of them.

Curly Bill made the introductions. Old Man Clanton, a Texan by way of California, was a surly, white-bearded, gimlet-eyed man with an overhanging belly. He sat with a rifle across his knees as though expecting a lawman's posse to show up at any moment. At mention of Ringo's name, he nodded.

"Heard of you. From down Mason County way, ain't you? Stirred up a mite of trouble with that iron of yours, they say. Got the law after you?"

Ringo felt an instant dislike for the crusty old outlaw. "Some things I keep to myself," he replied coldly.

Clanton twitched his shoulders. "Makes no mind to me. Always like to know where a man's standing."

The other Clantons—Ike, Phin, and the youngest, Billy—remained silent, merely nodded. The last man was Tom McLowry, a husky, red-faced rider with his gun hung low on his hip. He alone offered his hand.

"Pleased to meet you, Johnny," he said.

"Tom and his brother Frank own a ranch east of Tombstone, in the Sulphur Springs Valley," Curly Bill explained. "Makes a right handy place for us sometimes."

Ringo, bluff and to the point, turned to Hill. "Joe, I'm quitting. I'm riding on with Curly Bill and these men. Obliged to you for the job—"

Old Man Clanton twisted about slowly, looked Ringo up and down deliberately. "Who says you're riding with us?"

"I did," Brocius cut in. He was smiling, his broad white teeth gleaming beneath his black, down-curving mustache. But there was a hard glint in his eyes.

Clanton continued to study Ringo. "He half as mean as they say?"

"Maybe twice as much. I'll stack him up against any man here, or any we run across."

"Then I reckon it's all right for him to trail along. But he'll carry his own load. Won't have him leanin' on me—"

"I look after myself," Ringo said, Clanton's patronizing attitude rankling him. "Day will never come when I'll need you."

"Good enough," Old Man Clanton grunted.

Ringo swung his attention again to Hill. "Don't want to leave you shorthanded, Joe. If you say so, I'll hang around until you get another man."

"Forget it," the rancher said. "Drifters are coming by here all the time. I'll hire on the first likely-looking one I see. Pull out whenever you feel like it."

Clanton stroked his beard. "Sort of figured on staying the night, Joe, you having no objections."

"I ain't," Hill replied. "Make yourself at home. Beds in the back room and if there ain't enough there, some of you can sleep in the bunkhouse."

"We'll make out," McLowry said. "And it's right kind of you. Only thing, we don't want to cause you no trouble. That marshal at Lordsburg find out you put us up, could give you some problems."

Hill shrugged. "Law don't bother me and I don't bother it. Man's got a right to sleep whoever he wants in his own house, I reckon."

"And feed them, too?" Old Man Clanton added suggestively.

The rancher laughed. "Sure thing. I'll put the cook to work right now. Won't take long," he said, rising.

Ringo beckoned to Brocius and pivoted to the door. Outside, he said, "Might as well get my gear together. Thought maybe we could talk a bit while I'm doing it."

Curly Bill threw his arm across Ringo's shoulders. "Sure thing. Something special on your mind?"

Ringo moved slowly towards the bunkhouse. "This Clanton—the old man—how long you been running with him?"

"Year or two. He used to have a place at Fort Thomas.

Landed there after the vigilantes run him out of California for claim-jumping. Wife died up there and he sold out and moved to that ranch on the San Pedro. Brought the boys along with him." Curly Bill paused, grinned at Ringo. "Was I guessin', I'd say you don't cotton to him much."

"No, and I can't say as I care much for his boys, either."

Brocius' booming laugh echoed across the yard. "You ain't changed any, Johnny! Still right down the middle with everything plain black and white. But don't you fret none about the old man or his boys. They're good to ride the river with. Don't back off nothin'. And they know this country like the bottom of a whiskey glass. That old man could hide you out so's the devil himself would never find you."

They reached the long, low roofed building where Hill's hired hands quartered, and entered. Ringo said, "I'll take your word for it," and walking to his bunk, began to collect his belongings.

Brocius moved idly after him. He halted at a table near the head of Ringo's bed, picked up one of the half-dozen well-thumbed books that lay there and flipped through the pages slowly.

"Still doing all that reading, eh?"

"Man gets habits," Ringo replied.

"Like women and whiskey and stagecoach-robbing," Curly Bill said, laughing. "Only I never could see much fun in this reading thing."

Ringo favored Brocius with a slow grin. "I remember trying to explain that one night to you in Abilene. Got nowhere. Doubt if I'd have any better luck now."

"Probably right. Seems I got to feel or taste the kind of

fun I hanker for. You taking them along?"

Ringo said, "Sure, why not?"

"No reason. Want to be around to see the look on Old Man Clanton's face when he finds out about it, that's all. Some of the other boys, too."

Ringo paused. "They want to make something out of it, I'll be glad to explain—"

Curly Bill's booming laugh filled the room. "Yeah, I know the kind of explaining you do—'specially when you ain't in exactly the right mood! Now, I ain't telling you what to do, Johnny boy, but don't go taking the old man too hard. I'm not saying he ain't a lot of bite, but he is a lot of bark, and you kinda have to go along with him. He ain't used to no gentleman. He thinks anybody with learning and who changes his shirt more'n once a month is a dude tenderfoot."

Ringo considered that soberly. "I'll get along with him, but I won't take any rawhiding from him, either. Might be a good idea to have that understood right off the start."

Brocius glanced at Ringo's somber face. "Leave it to me," he said quickly. "Figured out a long time ago how to handle the old cuss and still come out ahead. Anyway, it'd be a hell of a thing to spill blood over."

Ringo said, "Good," and resumed his chore. "Way you sound, things must be pretty easy around here."

"Like falling drunk off a horse. And plenty of divvy-up when it's done with, too."

"Could use some cash," Ringo said, buckling down his saddlebag pouches. "Cowpunching pays mighty small money." His eyes swept the room, searched for items he might have missed. "Guess that does it. How about bunking out here with me tonight? Got a bottle stashed away. We could crack it open and hash over old times for a spell."

"Suits me to a T," Brocius said. "Soon as we eat we'll get at it. Like to know what you've been doing since we split up. Heard you had quite a ruckus down in Texas. Real surprise to me that a fine, upstandin' outlaw like you wasn't swingin' from a tree limb a long time ago!"

"Have to admit I had a few close ones," Ringo said, smiling. He started to add more, paused as the metal triangle at the back of the ranch house began to clang. "Grub's ready. Let's get a bite—then come on back here and start talking. There's a few questions I want to ask you. Little hard for me to understand how it is that you're still walking around free!"

3

From where he stood in the deep shadows of the canopy fronting the Oriental Saloon, John Ringo could look down Tombstone's main thoroughfare, Allen Street, and see just about everything of interest that was taking place. Although he had been in the turbulent little settlement on Goose Flats only a short time, he liked it and he had no regret for his decision to throw in with Curly Bill and the Clantons.

Tombstone was moving at high speed. There was endless excitement, a depthless store of wealth, and enough liquor flowing and poker to be played to satisfy even him. Ed Schieffelin's town, which had sprung to life in 1877, by that summer day in 1879 had vaulted to a seething population of well over a thousand souls, with more pouring in daily. If the rate of increase continued, it was estimated that in only two or three years, Tombstone—which an army wise-acre had prophesied would mark prospector Schieffelin's grave were he to venture into the area—would reach the staggering total of fifteen thousand persons!

And the cause of it all, silver, lay in limitless, inexhaustible quantities all through the surrounding hills. Everybody was getting rich—the mine owners, the miners, the merchants, the gamblers, the can-can girls, the politicians, and in particular the outlaws.

Things had changed somewhat, Curly Bill had explained to Ringo. While rustling cattle and horses was still lucrative, the Clanton-Brocius outfit, which numbered as high as a hundred men at times, bent its efforts now to stagecoach and bullion-wagon holdups. Both operated almost daily from Tombstone, destined for Tucson via Benson, or else rolled south for Bisbee. Often, on the return trip, they carried sizable payrolls.

In the beginning the mines simply used their own ore wagons, but as business mushroomed, the stage-line companies became interested and competition for hauling such shipments began. Bids were let and Wells Fargo got the nod. It made no difference to the Cowboys, as the outlaw element were commonly termed. They continued to ride fast and live high on the fat pickings. Every move by the mine operators was successfully circumvented—even when the frantic owners took to casting the silver bullion into three-hundred-pound blocks with the thought that such weighty ingots would prove too heavy and unwieldy for men on horseback to steal.

The outlaws solved the problem quickly. They simply drove, stagecoach and all, to a hiding place where they could manage the loot.

A man could about have his own way in Tombstone and that pleased John Ringo greatly. He could come and go as he pleased with little interference from the law. Of course there were the usual settlement ordinances, such as not wearing guns within the town limits, but few paid any attention to the regulation and there was no one with small enough regard for his life to try and enforce it.

Tombstone was a good town and Ringo liked it from the start. And he liked being again with Curly Bill, the one man he had ever trusted and considered a genuine friend. His feelings toward Old Man Clanton and his brood had not changed, however. He had his suspicions of all four. The two McLowrys were all right, as were most of the outfit. Many of them he knew from other places—Pony Deal, Frank Stilwell, Jim Crane, Harry Head, Bill Leonard, a couple more.

And there were those who were strangers to him, like Luther King, Jim Hughes, Hank Swilling, Milt Hicks, Johnny Barnes, the half-breed called Indian Charlie, Pete Spence, a youngster by the name of Billy Claiborne. He felt some small kinship with Claiborne, who had earlier come into the country with John Slaughter, but tiring of the everyday humdrum of cattle ranching, had cast his lot with the Cowboys.

There were many more whose names Ringo did not trouble himself to remember or even ascertain. And all, with the exception of Curly Bill, left him pretty much to his own devices, considering him aloof and sullen, and generally morose. That he might be a man of deep loneliness never occurred to any of them except, possibly, to Brocius, and he never offered any explanations or extended any apologies, simply withdrew into his shell of saturnine bitterness. They knew Ringo only as a dangerous, utterly reckless man best left alone at all times and more particularly when he was drinking—which was the major portion of the time.

Ringo turned, hearing the hard rap of boot heels behind him. Brocius, smiling broadly, pushed through the doors of the Oriental and halted at his shoulder.

"Picked me cleaner'n a turkey bone!" he said cheerfully. "Reckon I'll never learn."

An edged wind was blowing in across the whitish Tombstone hills from the Dragoons to the north, and the definite feel of winter was in the air. Ringo drew his coat tighter about his body. He nodded.

"Told you before, if you're bound to throw away your money, you might as well let me take it from you. I'll at least give you a run for it."

"A short run," Curly Bill said. "Funny thing—I know I can't beat a sharp like you but I always get the feeling I can win in a regular gambling hall. Never do. Seen any of the boys?"

"Only Stilwell and Swilling. They rode off toward Charleston about thirty minutes ago."

"Expect we'd better be high-tailin' it, too. The old man's got some scheme up his sleeve. Wants to hash it over."

"About time," Ringo murmured, stepping off the sidewalk. "Running low on cash."

"Low? I ain't seen you lose a hand of poker in a month! Figured you was rolling in cash, way you've been taking everybody around Charleston."

"Man makes money, he spends it," Ringo said laconically, and stopped short. His glance fastened upon a tall, square-faced man with deep-set eyes who had just emerged from the Cosmopolitan Hotel, a short distance down the street.

Brocius caught his intent gaze, followed it out with his own. He whistled at low pitch. "Wyatt Earp—sure as I'm a foot high! What's he doing here?"

"Wearing a badge," Ringo said "Expect we'd better see what kind."

They moved off through the ankle-deep dust together, two tall, powerfully built men walking shoulder to shoulder in that tight, forever ready manner of their kind. Earp saw them approaching, wheeled slowly around. The wind caught at the square corners of his coat, brushed them back, revealed the long-barreled pistol at his hip.

"Howdy, boys," he said as Ringo and Brocius came to a stop before him. "Figured I'd run into you two down here."

Ringo's eyes were on the star pinned to Earp's breast. " 'Deputy Sheriff,' " he quoted. "When did all this happen?"

"Few days ago in Tucson. Sheriff Shibell's having trouble collecting taxes around here. Gave me the job." He paused, stroked his full, sweeping mustache. "Don't get your dander up, boys I won't be bothering you."

"You won't," Ringo said softly.

Earp's bushy brows lifted. His jaw settled into a firm line. "We said our words in Wichita, Ringo," he stated in a quiet voice. "Let it end there."

Several passers-by, noting the meeting of the three men, had halted. They stood silent, watched and listened with interest. Somewhere a mine whistle blew.

"Fair enough, Wyatt," Brocius said. "What's behind us is gone. Taxes are something we sure don't owe, anyway."

"Then I'll not be calling on you. But you can tell Old Man Clanton and the McLowrys I'll be paying them a call. According to the records they never have got around to paying up."

"You tell them," Ringo said in that same soft, unrelenting way.

Earp studied the tall rider's features briefly. He nodded. "Be my job to. Well, see you boys again. We'll have to lift a drink together."

Brocius said, "Sure, sure thing—deputy."

Earp wheeled, moved off in the direction of Fourth Street. Ringo and Curly Bill watched him turn the corner, strike north toward Fremont, the avenue running parallel to Allen on the north.

"Beats me," Curly Bill said thoughtfully, "him taking a job as a tax collector. It sound right to you?"

John Ringo shook his head. "Quite a comedown for a big-time lawman like him. My hunch is there's more behind it."

"Meaning what?"

Ringo moved his shoulders. "Who knows what's in Earp's mind? He's a smart one."

"You pushed him a mite hard."

Ringo said, "One thing about Earp and me—we understand each other. I want to keep it that way."

"Expect you did, sure enough. Only there's an old sayin'—what is it?—something about letting sleeping dogs lay. Probably a good thing to keep in mind where Wyatt's concerned."

"He's not here to sleep," Ringo said shortly. "It's something else, and it's not tax collecting. But I guess all we can do is wait and see."

"Wait and see—that's sure it," Brocius echoed. "Going to have me some fun when I tell Old Man Clanton what he said. Sure ain't going to set much with him!"

"Nothing ever does," Ringo said dryly. "Come on, let's go see what he has on his mind."

4

It was near dark when they rode into Charleston. A small settlement on the San Pedro River, it was some nine miles southwest of Tombstone. The town was wide open and activity continued around the clock without letup. It was frequented mainly by the Cowboy element, a fact which prompted many to refer to it as Robbers Roost, an appellation most felt was not far wrong.

Clanton, with his three boys and a dozen other men, were in Barton's Saloon. When Ringo and Brocius entered, the white-bearded old renegade greeted them sourly.

"Was about to fix up this little fandango without you. Where you been?"

Curly Bill grinned. "Buckin' the tiger in Tombstone. Lost my shirt."

Ringo, obtaining a bottle from Barton, settled down at a

table somewhat apart, and, as usual, alone. When there was talking to be done with Old Man Clanton, he preferred that Curly Bill do it.

Clanton stroked his tobacco-stained, matted whiskers. "Man can be doin' that around here without traipsin' off across the country like a—"

Brocius continued to smile but it was faintly brittle along the edges. "Expect I'll go and come as I damn please. And while I'm thinking about it, we run into a lawman who says he's looking for you."

Clanton's small eyes narrowed. "What lawman?"

"Wyatt Earp. A real stem-winder from up Kansas way. Just took over a deputy job for Shibell at Tucson."

The old outlaw shifted indifferently. "Never heard of him. Why's he looking for me?"

"Taxes. Says you ain't paid any. You or the McLowrys, either. He's aiming to collect."

Clanton cackled. "Taxes! Well, he's sure welcome to try!"

"Only thing he'll ever collect around our place is bullets," Ike Clanton observed, removing a well-chewed cigar from between his teeth long enough to speak.

"And that's all he'll get," the old man added.

"Maybe so, but you won't catch me betting on it," Curly Bill said, winking at Ringo. "Earp ain't no wet-eared lawman that don't know up from down. He comes after taxes, he'll sure collect something he figures is worth while. Only thing is, we—Johnny and me—ain't so certain that's all he's hanging around for."

Old Man Clanton remained silent for a long minute. Then, "Forget 'im. Whatever he come for, if he fools with me, he'll wake up with a bellyful of lead. Now, you all listen close. Here's what I've been thinking. . . ."

John Ringo slouched in his chair, only half hearing. It was to be a holdup . . . Word had reached Clanton of a money shipment coming up from Bisbee. The old man had connections everywhere, it seemed. He always knew in advance when something especially good was to be aboard one of the stagecoaches.

Ringo's thoughts drifted to Wyatt Earp. He wondered again if the lawman's purpose in Tombstone was as he claimed or if there were other things brewing under cover. His last run-in with Earp had been in Wichita, and there was no good will between them—only a wary sort of respect. Earp had been going strong in Dodge City. Why had he left there? Why had he come to Tombstone?

A week later in Charleston he still pondered the problem. The holdup Old Man Clanton planned had failed. A decoy stage had been sent ahead by the mine owners and there had been no money on the one the Cowboys had halted. The long ride and cold wait in the windy canyons of the Mule Mountains had been for nothing. Ringo had sat in Barton's all that day following, angry and sullen, having only fair luck with the cards and mulling over his suspicions that Earp had had a part in the failure.

Near dark he had decided his fortunes might run better in Tombstone's Oriental Saloon and rising, had stalked wordlessly to his horse. Pony Deal halted him in the street.

"How about some shut-eye, Johnny?" he suggested in a careful, offhand way.

Ringo turned slowly, studied Deal narrowly. "You taking on the job of nursing me, Pony?"

Deal shrugged. "Hell, no. Point is we're both beat and not in such good shape. Walking around in the dark in Tombstone could be risky. Ike shooting that guard during the holdup's sort of got the town worked up."

"And maybe I ought to be careful, especially with Earp around, that it?"

"Didn't say that."

Ringo swung to his saddle. "I'm obliged to you, Pony," he said, his voice curt. "Been looking after myself for a long time. Day comes when I can't, I'll blow my brains out."

He whirled away from the hitch rack and started up the road at a gallop. He reached Tombstone in a few minutes and pulled up at one of his favorite saloons. Stiff and silent, he dismounted and pushed into the crowded room. Men, taking one look at his dark, set face, pulled back to let him pass and made room for him at the bar.

"Whiskey," he ordered.

The bartender slid a glass and bottle toward him, picked up the coin Ringo dropped, and moved farther back. Ringo poured himself a full measure of the raw liquor. He tipped it to his lips, drank it without pause. Refilling the tumbler, he glanced to his left. Louis Hancock, a slight acquaintance with whom he had played a few hands of poker, stood an arm's length away. Ringo nodded to him.

"Have a drink with me."

The bartender automatically shoved a second glass along the counter. Ringo filled it, pushed it at Hancock. The man shook his head, waggled the mug in his hand.

"Thanks, I'm drinking beer. Reckon I'll just stick with it."

The room hushed suddenly. Outside, the noise of the wind whipping against the frame buildings and tar-paper shacks was a dry, rasping sound.

"I'm asking you to drink with me," Ringo said softly. "One gentleman to another."

Hancock shifted his weight from his left to the right foot. He frowned. "Man's got a right to drink what he wants—"

"Take it," Ringo said, quietly insistent.

"You drink it," Hancock said flatly. "I'll do as I damn please—"

Ringo's ivory-handled Colts came up in a swift, smooth blur. The crash of the gunshot was a deafening explosion in the saloon. Hancock slammed back against the bar, setting off a bright tinkle of glassware. The man hung there momentarily and then slipped to the floor, dead.

The stunned silence held. Ringo finished his own drink in no haste, turned the glass bottom side up on the counter. He wheeled slowly on his heel, faced the men staring at him.

"I offer a man a drink, I expect him to accept," he said in distinct, well-spaced words. "Little rule of mine I'd like you all to remember."

He turned then, walked out into the street. Instantly voices broke out behind him in a rushing babble of words. Ringo gave it no thought, strode on through the lantern-lit darkness to the next saloon, where he knew he could find a card game in the progress.

There would be no repercussions. Hancock should not have refused the offer of the drink. It was a rule studiously observed throughout the frontier. And Hancock was armed, therefore it could not be termed murder. Had he not been wearing a gun it would have been a different story. Then John Ringo could have been held accountable for the man's death. The law in Tombstone, as in other like towns, drew a faint but definite line in such matters. Killing an unarmed citizen, or shooting in the back, was a crime that could lead to prosecution. Other than that a man was strictly on his own.

If there were any persons in Tombstone one hour after the Hancock incident who doubted or were unaware of the utter, pure violence that simmered within John Ringo, they no longer had reason to speculate on it. He had afforded a firsthand demonstration of his flashing temper. Thereafter Tombstoneites were to walk more lightly and respectfully in his presence.

5

John Ringo's decisive reaction to Hancock's refusal to drink with him had an even more far-reaching effect upon the town. On January 6, 1880, a group of the more prominent businessmen and citizens formed a committee and appointed ex-army officer Fred White to the position of town marshal. He was the first and they instructed him to bring some degree of law and order to the burgeoning community.

White went at it with a will, pressing particularly the ordinance prohibiting the carrying of firearms within the settlement limits. As a result, a great number of the lesser lights in the Brocius-Clanton Cowboy set confined their activities more to Charleston, the Clanton ranch on the San

Pedro, and the McLowry place in Sulphur Springs Valley.

Ringo's mistrust of Wyatt Earp increased steadily during this time and mounted higher when other members of the Earp family—brothers Virgil, Morgan, and Warren—drifted into town, to be followed shortly by Wyatt's close friend, gunfighter-gambler Doc Holliday.

To display his complete contempt for this growing array of lawmen, Old Man Clanton redoubled his depredations. The Cowboy gang began preying continually on the shipments of bullion and money, and broadened their interests to again include the cattle and horses of nearby ranchers.

Jim Hume, chief of the Wells Fargo office, immediately took countermeasures. He hired Wyatt Earp to ride shotgun on the important money shipments to and from Tucson. Wyatt, in turn, deputized Morgan Earp to assist. Capping it all, U.S. Marshal Crawly P. Dake arrived and appointed Wyatt as his deputy to serve in the Tombstone area of Pima County.

Ringo and Curly Bill knew then that they had been correct in their suspicions of Earp's true purpose in the settlement, but there was little they could do about it at the moment. To show their complete disregard of the family law combine, however, some of the Cowboys brazenly stole Wyatt's favorite horse and successfully kept it from him for some time. Matters grew warm during this interlude and there were open clashes on the streets but luckily it never got beyond that.

To the disappointment of the Citizens Safety Committee, White was unable to halt the shootings. Buckskin Frank Leslie, superior gun-slick and bartender par excellence for the Oriental Saloon, shot down Mike Kileen over the latter's estranged wife. Two or three more murders occurred, one a stand-and-deliver shoot-out in the center of Allen Street. Law with a stronger arm was needed.

The Committee, backed by sympathetic outlying communities, demanded the replacement of Sheriff Charlie Shibell, quartered at Tucson. They reasoned that the way to better enforcement was to start at the top. They proposed Bob Paul, a deputy U.S. marshal and shotgun messenger for the stage lines, as a replacement. Earp resigned as Shibell's deputy to support Paul. Shibell then pinned the star on John Behan, a man known to be friendly with the Cowboys, as Earp's successor.

Thus matters backfired completely for the Citizens Safety Committee, and called for an immediate celebration on the part of the Brocius-Clanton crowd. A number of them rode in to take over. They met no opposition and for two days and nights they kept the town in an uproar, with Curly Bill leading the pack. On the evening of October twenty-seventh, Marshal Fred White, with Behan and his associates looking on, appealed to Wyatt Earp for aid in taming the rioters.

Earp agreed and the two men began. They closed in upon Curly Bill, first of all. In the scuffle that ensued, White was shot accidentally by Brocius and fatally wounded. As he was being carried away, Earp turned upon Brocius and viciously pistol-whipped him during the process of arrest. He jailed him, then proceeded to round up more of the Cowboys, including Pony Deal, the two McLowrys, Ike and Billy Clanton, to mention the more prominent. All were locked up and charged with carrying firearms inside the city limits.

The remainder of the celebrants faded off into the night to resume their activities in Charleston. There, John Ringo, sitting in on a poker game, listened to an account of what had taken place in Tombstone. When the report was finished, he rose to his feet and started for the door of the saloon.

"How about finishing the game?" one of the card players called after him.

Ringo paused, glanced back over his shoulder. "I've got some business with Wyatt Earp," he said, and moved on into the crisp night.

As he rode toward the settlement there was no doubt in John Ringo's mind that Curly Bill was a victim of Earp's cunning; it had all been a put-up job—and the time to settle with the lawman was at hand. He had been expecting something such as this ever since Earp had turned up in Tombstone. Now the cards were out on the table.

He reached the edge of town, swung into Allen Street. He pulled his horse down to a slow walk. There were many persons abroad. They drew off to the sides immediately when they saw him approaching. He moved down the center of the dusty thoroughfare, his glance swinging from one building to another as he sought the marshal.

He came to the end of the street, angled toward the jail, where another deputy leaned against the hitch rack. He halted, placed his hard gaze on the man.

"I'm looking for Wyatt. You seen him?"

The deputy took one look at Ringo's grim farce and summoned Chief Deputy Sheriff Behan. The lawman, a short, stocky Missourian with friendly, round eyes, dark hair, and a flowing mustache, came from the interior of the jail and stepped up to Ringo's side.

"What's this all about, Johnny?"

"I'm going to settle with Wyatt Earp for what he did to Curly Bill. Any idea where I can find him?"

Behan hesitated for a moment, then, "No, I sure don't. You think this is the thing to do?"

Ringo's voice was cold. "Wyatt asked for it. He's been waiting for a chance to get at Curly and me. I don't figure to let him get away with it."

Behan shook his head. "I don't owe Earp anything but I think you ought to get the straight of it. Curly Bill's all right. He got roughed up a bit but he's not hurt any. He'll be fine after he sleeps off all that whiskey he put away."

"Which will be just in time for Wyatt to haul him up before a judge and get the book thrown at him for shooting Fred White!" Ringo added bitterly. "This thing was made to order for Earp. It ought to suit him perfectly! But I'm not letting it go that far. I'm settling with him before he can pull it off."

Behan laid his hand on Ringo's knee. "Easy, Johnny. That's not the way it's going to be. Curly shot White, sure, and it's bad. But it wasn't exactly Curly Bill's fault. Fred cleared him of it. Said he had no business grabbing his gun by the barrel."

"Won't mean a thing to Wyatt. He'll still hang it on Curly—"

"Not likely. Earp confirmed what Fred White said."

Ringo frowned. "That it was an accident?"

"Right. I was there and heard him. There won't be any charges."

John Ringo was silent for a long minute. Finally he

shrugged. “Don’t know whether I can trust Earp or not. Expect I’d still better have a talk with him.”

Behan said, “You can trust me, Johnny. I personally guarantee Curly Bill will go free in the morning, along with the rest of the boys. And forget Earp—it’s not worth it. Go on back to Charleston—there’ll come a better time.”

Ringo considered that briefly, nodded. “All right, Sheriff. I’m trusting you,” he said, and pulled away from the lawman.

White died from his wound after officially exonerating Brocius of all blame. All those who had been jailed with him by Earp were levied a small fine and released. As John Behan had promised, things were quickly back to normal and Wyatt Earp made no further trouble.

Again outlawry swung into full blush, with the stage lines and ranchers paying heavy toll to the masked riders who swept across the hills. It was a strange situation. Even the rawest tenderfoot newcomer to the settlement knew the identities of the bandits and likely could point them out by name as they swaggered down Tombstone’s streets, spending the loot from their latest escapade. But the lack of absolute proof and the hard pressure of fear kept most lips sealed. Only a few had the courage to cry out, such as Editor Clum of the newly founded *Epitaph*, and he did it with prudent generality.

With matters going well, Old Man Clanton decided to further broaden his scope. He turned over the ranch on the San Pedro to his three sons and moved to a new location in New Mexico’s Animas Valley, a short mile north of the Mexican border. This would enable him to handle rustled stock with greater ease, he said. A new town, quickly a favored place for the Cowboys, came into being on the eastern slopes of the Chiricahuas. It was named Galeyville, and Curly Bill, forging more and more to the front as the leader of the gang, began to make it his headquarters.

With White dead, Virgil Earp was appointed to fill out the unexpired term in the hope that he could keep some sort of lid on the explosive unrest in Tombstone until a new marshal could be elected in December—two months off.

Aided by brothers Wyatt and Morgan, Virgil proved to be an iron-fisted lawman, so much so that he not only further antagonized the Cowboy element to a dangerous peak and multiplied their hatred for the Earp name, but also turned a large number of ordinary citizens against him.

When the results were in at the polls, he had been defeated by Ben Sippy, an in-between-the-factions candidate with no particular ability for anything. Bob Paul, however, was elected to replace Charlie Shibell as Pima County's sheriff. But victory for the Safety Committee was short-lived. Shibell protested the results after hearing of certain maneuverings by Wyatt Earp in Paul's behalf. Election officials in Prescott then ordered Shibell to remain in office, declaring a *status quo,* until they could investigate the matter.

This confusion permitted the Cowboys to take a firmer grip on Tombstone and gain almost complete control of the country surrounding the settlement. And it brought John Ringo into headlong collision with his old enemy, Wyatt Earp.

6

The game broke up in the cold, gray light of morning. Ringo and Curly Bill, having played in another game elsewhere in the saloon, had finished earlier. They now watched with interest the final hand in the card duel between the little ferret-faced gambler John O'Rourke—commonly known as Johnny-Behind-the-Deuce because of his propensity for backing that low card in faro—and Henry Schneider, chief engineer for the Tombstone Mining & Milling Corporation.

Schneider played badly and O'Rourke, always a poor loser and a worse winner, threw down the winning hand. He began to rake in the money with greedy haste, smirking broadly at the engineer.

"Come around again when you want a lesson in poker playin'," he said. "And bring plenty of cash. Always a cinch to pluck a greenhorn like you."

Schneider's temper flared. His face flushed a bright red. "No two-bit tinhorn's talking to me like that!" he shouted, and kicked back his chair.

Johnny-Behind-the-Deuce drew quickly. His gun roared and Schneider, in the act of reaching for a knife in his coat pocket, staggered and fell, instantly dead.

Ringo and Brocius, along with a dozen or so more spectators, rushed forward. From the street came Constable George McKelvy, saloonkeeper J. B. Ayers and other men attracted not by the gunshot, common enough in Charleston, but by the shouts of a man who raced through the doorway yelling that Schneider had been killed.

O'Rourke was not liked. Schneider, on the other hand, had been one of the regular crowd, friendly to all, and had played cards with most everyone. Curly Bill grabbed the tinhorn by the collar.

"Get a rope!" he ordered. "We'll teach this jasper a lesson!"

The cry was taken up immediately. O'Rourke, panic-stricken, jerked free of Curly Bill's fingers. He dodged by Ringo and several other men, lunged for the door. McKelvy was just entering.

"They're going to lynch me!"

McKelvy shoved O'Rourke into the street. He drew his gun, waved it threateningly at the crowd. Backing out slowly onto the gallery, he pulled the door shut.

"Get to the jail!" he yelled, wheeling to the gambler.

He locked Johnny-Behind-the-Deuce in a cell and walked back into the open. The bartender met him.

"Better get that tinhorn out of town," the man warned. "Ringo and Curly Bill are getting the boys together. They're going to string him up sure as hell!"

McKelvy knew he didn't stand a chance against a lynch mob. They would storm his flimsy jail, easily take it apart piece by piece and get their man. He hurried to where he had left his team of mules and buckboard. He brought the rig around and loaded Johnny-Behind-the-Deuce on the seat.

"If we can make it to Tombstone," he said, whirling on into the street, "you'll be all right."

Ringo and the mob, gathered in front of Quinn's Saloon, saw them wheel onto the Tombstone road. There was an immediate shift toward their horses and in moments the crowd was mounted and thundering off into McKelvy's dust.

The mules had a good start but they were no match for horses. Two thirds of the way to Tombstone, the lynch mob, with Ringo and Brocius at the head, pulled into shooting range. Guns opened up and bullets began to pock the road behind the vehicle.

"We ain't going to make it!" O'Rourke cried to McKelvy. "Swing over toward McCann's place. I'll jump and run for it."

McCann's Saloon was a quarter mile distant. McKelvy glanced over his shoulder. Ringo and the others were less than three hundred yards back.

"You'd never reach it," he said.

He looked ahead. A rider had appeared on the crest of the hill up which the tiring mules labored. McKelvy stared hard. It was Virgil Earp. Hope lifted within the constable. He half stood in the swaying buckboard, waved for Earp to come nearer. Earp put spurs to his horse, rushed downgrade to meet them. With the yelling, shooting mob giving chase, he knew instantly something was wrong. He wheeled in beside McKelvy.

"What's the trouble?"

Without slowing the mules, the lawman said, "Ringo and that mob's out to lynch this man. I'm trying to get him to Tombstone where he'll be safe."

Earp did not hesitate. He motioned to O'Rourke. "Jump on behind me," he said. "I'll get you there."

The gambler leaped from the buckboard onto Earp's horse. The mob was now dangerously close and pulling up fast. Earp dug his heels into the flanks of his mount and the animal surged away. Immediately he began to draw off from Ringo and the others. The best was behind their horses, which had come a long, upgrade seven miles from Charleston at top speed.

Virgil, with Johnny-Behind-the-Deuce clinging to him, reached Tombstone only minutes ahead of the mob. He went straight to the Wells Fargo office, where he thought Wyatt most likely would be found. Morgan also was there. Virgil hastily related the story of what was taking place. At that moment the pound of running horses sounded on Toughnut Street, one block away.

"That's them!" Virgil finished.

Wyatt reached for a double-barreled shotgun standing in the rack. "No time left to reach the jail," he said to his brother. "Take O'Rourke down the street to Vogan's Bowling Alley. Best place I can think of to make a stand."

Vogan's was at the beginning of the next block, a long, narrow building protected on either side by other structures. Virgil wheeled off at once. At that moment Jim Earp, another brother, who had arrived recently, came up.

"There's a big mob from Charleston down on Toughnut," he said. "Say they're going to lynch some tinhorn gambler who murdered one of their friends. They're recruiting more help from the miners."

Wyatt spun to Morgan. "You and Virgil get around in back of Vogan's. Not much room there and you can hold them off easy if they come that way. I'll look after the front."

He swung back to the several men who had gathered before the stage-line office. "Grab yourselves guns. You're deputized."

He started at a trot for the entrance to Vogan's, the deputies falling in behind him. They had barely reached the bowling alley when the howling mob, led now not only by Ringo and Curly Bill but also by Richard Gird, one of the prominent mine owners in the area, broke into Allen Street.

"Where'd they take him?" Curly Bill yelled at a bystander.

"Into Vogan's," the man replied.

The shouting, milling crowd swerved, flowed in toward the bowling alley, and came to a halt. Earp and his hastily acquired deputies, shotguns in hand, formed a line before the door.

"Nobody gets by me," Earp said, lifting his weapon menacingly.

Far back in the mob a voice shouted, "Rush 'em! There ain't enough of 'em to hold us back!"

Earp faced the crowd coolly. He let his glance touch Ringo, Curly Bill, and then halt on Gird. The mine owner was an influential citizen, one-time partner of the town's founder, Ed Schieffelin.

"Surprised to see you running with a bunch like this, Mr. Gird."

The mine owner, his face taut, said, "That tinhorn—he murdered Henry Schneider. I figure a hanging is what he needs!"

Earp nodded. "Agreed, but by the law. And it's my job to see it's done that way."

A yell arose from the crowd and it pushed forward. "Get the tinhorn! String him up!"

"Don't stand there yammerin'! Tromp over them

deputies!"

Earp studied Gird. "If I have to shoot to stop this mob, I'll do it. And you'll be the first one to get it."

Another surge from the depths of the crowd shoved the mine owner, Ringo, Brocius, and others in the front line closer. Earp and his deputies swung their weapons back and forth slowly.

"You can't shoot us all!" a voice in the depths of the pack cried.

"No, but we'll get ten or twelve of you with the buckshot in these scatterguns," Earp replied. He had not taken his eyes off Gird.

"Think that over, Dick. Is the tinhorn worth it?"

Ringo moved forward a step. Immediately Earp brought the muzzle of his weapon to bear on the tall rider. "No closer, Johnny. And think twice—you wouldn't have a chance."

Ringo paused. He was fast, and he knew his own capabilities. But no man could reach, draw, and beat the blast of a shotgun already cocked and leveled at him.

Dick Gird broke the sudden tension. He turned about, lifted his arms above his head. "Let Earp have him, boys. He's not worth any of us getting killed over."

Gird started pushing his way back through the crowd. For a time no one moved and then the rest of the men wheeled, followed. Ringo and Curly Bill stared at Earp and his deputies for several moments and then they, too, spun about and headed for Toughnut Street.

Behind them Earp said, "Somebody get me a horse and buggy. I'm taking the prisoner to Tucson for trial." He lifted his glance to Deputy Sheriff John Behan and Town

Marshal Ben Sippy, standing a few yards away. They had taken no part in protecting O'Rourke, simply stood by and watched. "He'd stand no chance around here."

Ringo, overhearing, halted. He looked at Brocius. "We can head them off before they reach Benson," he said suggestively.

Curly Bill grinned. "Naw, let them go. Fun's all over now. Let's head for Galeyville."

7

Important changes were under way at that time in Prescott, Arizona's capital. Powerful political factions, aware of the limitless riches in the Tombstone area, prevailed upon the Legislature to create a new county in that southeastern corner of the territory, with Tombstone as the seat of government.

The lawmakers carved some six thousand square miles out of existing Pima County and named it Cochise. The new county had its birth in January, 1881, and immediately created a need for governing officials. Since no election could be held until November, 1882, officers would therefore have to be appointed.

Deputy John Behan announced immediately that he would seek the position of sheriff. The Law and Order Party, the Citizens Committee, and certain other groups chose to back Wyatt Earp. The Brocius-Clanton clique lined up behind Behan, who had been friendly to them in the past, and quickly set to work doing what they could to obtain the appointment for the deputy.

The pros and cons involving the two men rocked Tombstone for several days, with the local newspapers taking a big hand in it. The *Epitaph* and its editor, John C. Clum, stood by Wyatt Earp. Harry Woods, of the *Nugget*, pegged tirelessly for Behan. Electioneering, of the style generally reserved for presidential elections, was the order of the day. Petitions, affidavits, requests, and recommendations flowed steadily into Prescott from the residents of the new county.

It fell upon John Ringo to give it the dramatic, almost tragic, touch. With Curly Bill and several other members of the Cowboy set, he swaggered one day up and down Allen Street expressing his opinion freely as to the abilities and qualifications of the candidates. Inwardly he still glowed with suspicion and hatred for Earp and when he saw the lawman, late that cold morning, standing in front of a saloon talking with Mayor Thomas, he deliberately swung from his path and accosted him.

"Earp," he said, "I know how we can settle this matter without any further argument. And sooner or later you and I are coming to a showdown, anyway. How about stepping out into the middle of the street with me?"

Morgan and Virgil Earp, and Doc Holliday, lounging against the wall of the saloon a few paces behind Wyatt, came to attention. They spread out quietly. Directly across the street facing them, Brocius, the two McLowrys, Ike and Billy Clanton watched with close interest.

Earp said, "Forget it, Ringo. You're drunk."

The tall outlaw shook his head. "Step out here. We'll mark off ten paces and shoot it out, man to man. That ought to be fair."

Earp's face was stiff. "Johnny, you know me well

enough to realize I don't go for sucker plays. I'd be a damn fool, running for sheriff like I am, to take you on in a shoot-out right here in the middle of town. Move on, sleep off that load of whiskey you're carrying, and forget it."

Earp spun on his heel, walked into the saloon. Doc Holliday eased forward to the edge of the walk, eyes bright and expectant. Ringo's attention swiveled to him.

"You game, Holliday?"

The cadaverous, hollow-cheeked gambler nodded. "For anything, Johnny—any time."

Ringo raised his left hand slowly, plucked a handkerchief from the breast pocket of his coat. He extended it toward Holliday.

"Here, take hold of this. We don't need but three feet."

Holliday grasped the corner of the cloth. "I'm your boy," he murmured.

The two men squared off, hands poised above their weapons. At that moment, Mayor Thomas pushed in between them.

"Hold on here, you two! There'll be no handkerchief duel while I'm around. There's been enough killing in this town without you adding to it."

Thomas turned his back to Ringo, placed his hands on Holliday's shoulders, wheeled him about and shoved him toward the saloon door. "Go inside and cool off, Doc. And you," he added, glaring at Ringo, "keep moving. If you don't, I'll have Ben Sippy jail you for disturbing the peace."

Ringo smiled faintly at Thomas, then shrugged and strode off to rejoin Curly Bill and the other Cowboys. In a group they sauntered on down the street.

John Behan drew the nod from Prescott and became the

sheriff of Cochise County, with headquarters in Tombstone. He immediately appointed Harry Woods, editor of the *Nugget*, his undersheriff. For deputies he selected Dave Campbell, William Breakenridge, Frank Hereford, Dave Neagle, Lance Perkins, and in a candid display of appreciation for the Cowboys' efforts on his behalf, Frank Stilwell, a member of the Brocius-Clanton gang.

When the news reached Galeyville that Behan was victorious and in full command of the law, a small celebration was set off. John Behan was their friend and the appointment of Frank Stilwell was significant.

"We've got it made," Curly Bill said. "The town's ours any time we want it."

Ringo wasn't so certain. "Don't forget Earp. He's still there, playing at deputy U.S. marshal and riding guard for Wells Fargo. He also has all his brothers hanging around, along with Doc Holliday."

Old Man Clanton, sunk deep in a chair, glanced up. "You turning tail on Earp?"

Ringo's taut face shifted to Clanton. "No, not to him or any other man. But I know Wyatt. He won't quit, not if he's working for something else. Just because Behan beat him out for that appointment he won't stop. You're a fool if you count him short."

Clanton grunted. "Day's coming when I'll settle with him."

"Take a better man than you," Ringo snapped, and swung off toward a back room of the saloon, where Dave Estes and several men awaited him to begin a poker game.

He was still angry as he sat down at the table and called for the dealer to begin. He was usually expert with cards but that day and evening nothing fell right for him, or for Estes, either. At midnight they arose, both near broke, and pulled out of the game. Ringo, carrying his usual quota of liquor but still in absolute control of his faculties, motioned for Estes to follow him.

They went outside to where the horses were stabled and began to saddle up. Ringo paused at the chore.

"Dave, I've got a hunch we've been played for suckers in there," he said.

Estes shook his head. That anyone would try to cold-deck John Ringo, one of the best poker players and deadliest gunmen in the country, was inconceivable.

"Didn't see anything wrong, Johnny," he said, protesting mildly.

"I think there was," Ringo replied. "And I mean to set it straight."

Finished throwing on their gear, they led the horses around to the front of the deserted saloon. Ringo drew his gun and, with Estes behind him, entered the back room. One of the players was just fanning out his cards for the others to see.

"Four aces—reckon that beats anything."

"Not quite," Ringo drawled, and stepped up to the table. "Where I come from a six-shooter beats everything!"

He leaned forward, gathered up the currency and coins scattered in front of the men, stuffed them into his pockets.

"I figure this about makes us square," he said, and started backing for the door. "Best advice I can give you now is to sit tight. Don't try to be heroes."

The men at the table said nothing, made no move to interfere. John Ringo, they knew, was a man you didn't cross regardless of the situation. When he was gone they settled back in relief, laughed it off. It was a good joke, they felt—all but Webb, the man who had been holding the four aces. The more he thought about it the angrier he became. He rode into Tombstone the following day and filed a robbery charge with Sheriff Behan against Ringo.

The lawman sought to discourage Webb from so dangerous a move but the outraged poker player stood firm and in the end the complaint was duly lodged. Deputy Billy Breakenridge was sent to Galeyville to arrest Ringo.

He found Ringo in his cabin, withdrawn as usual from other members of the gang, and reading one of his books. Breakenridge, knowing he trod on dynamite, proceeded with caution.

"Johnny, there's a little trouble in town."

Ringo studied the lawman for a moment. "So? What does it have to do with me?"

"Everything. The sheriff sent me out here to tell you about it."

"All right, go ahead. I'm listening."

"It's that fellow Webb," Breakenridge blurted. "He swore out a warrant for your arrest. Robbery."

The single fact that Breakenridge worked for John Behan was probably all that kept him from being shot down where he stood.

"Arrest me for getting even with those highbinders?" Ringo shouted, leaping to his feet. "That damn Webb—"

"Wasn't anything we could do but serve the warrant," Breakenridge said.

Ringo's soaring temper cooled. He walked to the door, looked out into the street. "Anybody else know about this?"

"Only the sheriff and me. And Webb, of course."

"Keep it that way. Ride back into town. I'll come in later."

"But I'm supposed—"

"You tell Behan I said I'd come in. My word's good with him."

Breakenridge sighed. He had no alternative but to accept Ringo's promise. He returned to Tombstone and reported to the sheriff.

"Ringo will be here," the lawman said. "He's one man you can figure won't go back on his word."

Late the afternoon of the next day Ringo rode into the settlement and presented himself at the sheriff's office.

"Glad you showed up," Behan said. "Expected you a little earlier."

Ringo shrugged. "Said I'd be here. And there wasn't any time set. What's next?"

"Too late to do anything about bail today. Get yourself a room across the street and I'll hunt up a lawyer. He can arrange bail and you can go on back to Galeyville in the morning. I'll have to ask you not to leave town until the bail is put up."

Ringo said, "I won't. But get busy finding that lawyer."

The attorney was located and the legal wheels were set to turning. Later on that evening another of Behan's deputies came in. Earp and several of his friends were going after Curly Bill, he said. Brocius had been accused of robbing a stage, singlehanded. He was reported to be in Charleston. The Earp party planned to move in on him at daylight.

In the meantime Ringo's lawyer had succeeded in

raising money estimated to be sufficient to cover the bail. He entered the jail and faced Behan.

"Got it all ready," he said. "When court convenes in the morning I'll be there with the cash."

Ringo, alarmed that Brocius would be taken unaware by the Earps, asked impatiently, "Any need for me to wait?"

Behan shook his head. "Not necessary. Long as I know you'll be represented before the judge and have the bail money ready, you won't have to appear personally."

"Then turn me loose," Ringo said.

He went immediately to the livery stable, and mounting his horse, rode for Charleston. It was near daylight and he knew he could not be far ahead of the Earp posse. He reached the settlement, and after warning Curly Bill, who was dozing in Barton's Saloon, returned to the bridge that spanned the San Pedro River. There he awaited the lawman.

Earp arrived a short time later. With him were his brother Virgil and Doc Holliday. Ringo held back until they were at the bridge approach and then stepped into view.

"No use going any farther, Wyatt," he said. "Curly Bill has gone."

Earp and the others pulled up short. Virgil swore vividly and Holliday watched with that secret half smile, half sneer of his.

"Thought you were locked up in Behan's jail," Wyatt said, his voice hard-edged and faintly surprised.

Ringo's question came back sharp and quick. "How did you know about that? You have something to do with it?"

"Just heard about it, that's all," Earp said evenly. "You say Curly Bill's gone?"

"He's gone. I'm the only one around—and I'm right here."

Earp was silent, apparently considering the odds, the necessity. Suddenly he shook his head, wheeled about. The others, without looking at Ringo, followed. The tall outlaw waited on the bridge until there was no doubt of their leaving, and then dropped back to Charleston for a bite of breakfast and a few hours' sleep.

Shortly after noon, he mounted and rode across the Sulphur Springs Valley into the foothills of the Chiricahuas, and Galeyville, where he knew Curly Bill had gone.

Brocius was waiting for him. "Obliged to you, Johnny, for tipping me off. Shape I was in, I couldn't have done much good against the Earps."

"Virgil and Doc Holliday were with Wyatt," Ringo said. "They were loaded for bear."

"Thing that gets me," Brocius said, scratching at his ear, "is how'd they know I was there? I'd swear nobody saw me slip in."

"Might be something we ought to look into," Ringo said.

"For a fact. Main thing I wanted to tell you, however, is that it looks like you got Johnny Behan in a spot of trouble."

Ringo frowned. "Me? How?"

"Pete here just come up from Tombstone. Appears Earp had it all fixed with the judge to not let you out on bail. When Behan didn't produce you in court this morning the judge raised all kinds of hell with him. Said he had no business turning you loose."

"That lawyer figured it was all right," Ringo said. "And it's been done before."

"Sure, and it'll be done that way again, only this time Wyatt had a hand in it. Had a reason for wanting you kept under lock and key."

"I'm seeing through a few things now," Ringo said. "Guess I spoiled his little plan for nailing you to the wall. Where do we stand now—with Behan, I mean?"

"The judge give him until tomorrow to have you in court. Expect it could put him in big trouble, if he don't."

"I'll be there," Ringo said.

"That judge could be mad enough to throw you in the jug for a few months, maybe even a year."

Ringo grinned. "He does, I'll be expecting you and a few of the boys down to get me out. Main thing, we can't leave Behan in a fix because of the favor he did for me."

"Know that. But what about Wyatt? He's going to be plenty hot, too."

"Earp doesn't worry me any. He's been hot before."

"Maybe so, but just for luck some of the boys and me will ride in with you."

Court had already convened when John Ringo loped into Tombstone the next morning. He pulled up before the jail, dismounted. Breakenridge appeared in the doorway.

"Where's Behan?" Ringo asked.

The deputy grinned. "Over at the courthouse trying to explain to the judge why you aren't here. Come on, let's get over there."

They hurried to the courtroom. As they entered the jurist was lecturing the sheriff sternly on the proper procedures to be observed by his office, and the fallacy of relying upon an outlaw's word.

"No need to worry, your honor," Breakenridge said,

interrupting. "Here's the prisoner, John Ringo."

The judge paused. Behan, relief showing on his round face, wheeled about. After a minute the hearing went ahead as scheduled. Ringo was fined for his crime, released, and the matter was closed.

8

The chasm between Old Man Clanton on one side, and John Ringo, Curly Bill, and several of the gang on the other, widened considerably in that spring of 1881. On the night of March fifteenth, four of the clan, operating entirely on their own and without Clanton's knowledge and sanction, attempted to hold up a bullion stage for Benson.

The shipment of silver, valued at eighty thousand dollars, was in the care of Bob Paul, still serving as shotgun messenger for the stage company while he waited for the authorities to decide on Sheriff Shibell's appeal. The driver of the coach was Bud Philpot, an old hand at the business.

Near Drew's Ranch on the Benson road, three bandits stepped suddenly out of the darkness and ordered the stage to halt. Paul ignored the command, yelled for Philpot to whip up the horses. The coach whirled away and the outlaws opened fire. Philpot was killed instantly and a passenger by the name of Roerig was dead a few minutes later. Paul, recovering the reins dropped by Philpot, managed to get the horses under control and drove the stage on to Benson, where he wired Wyatt Earp the details of the holdup.

Earp had acted immediately. He deputized Virgil and

Morgan, along with Bat Masterson, who happened to be working in the Oriental at the time, and Marshal Williams, the Wells Fargo agent. They set out on the trail of the outlaws and soon ran down Luther King, who admitted to being a member of the party but claimed to have done none of the shooting. He had served only as the horse holder, he claimed. Under pressure he finally named the other bandits as Bill Leonard, Jim Crane, and Harry Head.

King was turned over to Sheriff Behan, since he had proper jurisdiction in the crime, and this resulted in a new furor in Tombstone when King subsequently escaped, apparently with ease. Meanwhile Earp and his posse continued to hunt the other three men, who eventually gave him the slip by ducking across the border into Mexico.

Old Man Clanton took the attempted robbery hard. He had not been aware of the bullion shipment and the four men had acted without his knowledge.

"If I'da known about it," he declared, "it would've been done right. No messin' it up like they did, and we'da been splitting that eighty thousand instead of just setting here wishing."

"Nobody knew about the money," Curly Bill said. "Expect it showed up all at once and the boys, being handy, jumped at the chance. Wasn't much else they could do but make a try."

"Could have sent for me," Clanton muttered, in his dry, dissatisfied way.

"Maybe there wasn't time," Brocius said. "Anyway, it's done and there ain't no use squawkin' about it. Point is we've got to give Leonard and the boys some help until it blows over."

"Ain't going to blow over," Clanton insisted. "Two killings—makes Earp want them three bad. Now, I figure this is the time to play it real smart."

Brocius, standing with his elbows hooked on the edge of the bar, cocked his head to one side. "Meaning?"

"Just this. We're going to set ourselves in good with Earp and the Wells Forgo people. We're going to string them along, and the next time an eighty-thousand-dollar-or-so shipment goes out, we'll nab it pretty as you please."

"Sounds fine but how you figure to do it?"

"Easy. Fix it up so's Earp can lay his hands on Leonard and them others. We'll be hearing from them soon and when we do, we tip off Earp."

Ringo, sitting at a table in the back of the room, came forward off his chair. "You'll do what?"

Old Man Clanton eyed him coldly. "You heard me. You ain't deaf. We're making a deal with Earp. We'll set it up so's he can grab Leonard and Jim Crane and Harry Head. That way we'll not only collect the two-thousand-dollar reward Wells Fargo is paying for each one of them, but we'll be putting ourselves in solid with the Earp bunch."

"I'll be no part of a double-cross like that!" Ringo said, his voice flat.

Brocius lifted his hand, motioned Ringo back. "Earp won't swallow it. If you're thinking you can make him believe we've swapped over and are working his side, you're plumb loco."

"He'll believe it," Old Man Clanton said, "once we hand him Leonard and the others. Far as I'm concerned," he added, looking again at Ringo, "you don't have to take no part in it. Goes for anybody else. Some of you don't like the way I'm runnin' things, pull out."

"Well, I'm not pulling out," Curly Bill said, settling back against the bar, "and you can count me out on the kind of a deal you're cooking up, too. Those boys are friends of mine."

"Being friends don't count for nothin'," Clanton said. "Not at a time like this. They done a fool stunt and they got to pay for it. And if we play along with Earp and his bunch, it'll take the heat off us, make things easy for us next time a big haul comes along."

"Way I look at it, money ain't worth that much," Brocius said. "Expect you'll find a few more of the boys who feel the same as me and Ringo."

A murmur of agreement ran through the men gathered in the saloon. Clanton allowed his gaze to drift over them, his small, pale eyes snapping with scorn.

"Suit yourself," he said finally, "but I reckon I can find enough that still figure I call the shots for this outfit and who'll string along with me. Now, Ike, you ride into town. See Earp. First thing, find out if that reward for them boys means dead or alive. Then tell him we want to make a deal."

Ringo, his face dark, moved up to front Clanton. "Ike's going nowhere," he said "He or nobody else—not if it's to see Earp."

Curly Bill pulled away from the bar. He laid a broad hand on the tall man's shoulder, ducked his head at the door. "Forget it, Johnny. Come on out in the yard. Couple of things I want to tell you."

Ringo followed Brocius into the open. When they were well out of earshot, Curly Bill said, "Don't get so all-fired het up at the old man. Let him have his way. He's about done for. Besides, Earp won't fall for a yarn like that. And even if he does, how can the old man deliver? Bill and the others are down in Mexico."

"They could come back."

"Not if we get word to them to stay put. I figure to send Indian Charlie and tell them what Clanton's scheming up and warn them to lay low until they heard from me again."

Ringo considered for a long minute. "All right, but can't say as I like it much. Seems to me it would be better to stop the old man before he makes the first move."

Curly Bill winked. "I'm looking at it the other way. I've got a hunch the whole blamed thing's going to blow up in his face. And that's what I'm waiting for. I don't want to see the outfit bust up, like it maybe will if we just horse the old man out.

"Smart thing to do is let him cut his own throat Then the boys will stick together. We fight him over this, it could split things wide open. You got to remember them three boys of his will stand by him. So will the McLowrys and a good many more. And we'd be fools to be bucking each other. That would suit Earp and his crowd to a T. Just you forget it, Johnny boy. Let the old goat think he's having his way—and don't worry none about Bill Leonard and the rest. I'll warn them."

Ringo nodded. "All right, Curly. I'll go along with you. But if anything happens to those three because of Old Man Clanton, he'll answer to me!"

"And to me," Brocius said. "It won't, though. I'm promising you that."

Clanton made his deal with Wyatt Earp and the Wells

Fargo office, doing his negotiating through Ike, Frank McLowry and Joe Hill. The reward was to be two thousand dollars for each of the three bandits who participated in the holdup and killings. It was payable dead or alive.

Clanton contracted to lead Earp and a posse to Leonard, Head, and Crane as soon as they could be located. They were then in Mexico, as Earp knew, but word would be sent down advising them they now were safe and that they could return to Galeyville. Earp would be kept posted at all times.

When Ike and the others returned to report the successful completion of their mission, Old Man Clanton was pleased.

"Mighty fine," he said, rubbing his gnarled hands together. "It's working out good. I already sent word to Leonard for them to meet us at Rabbit Springs. Told him we was figuring to hold up the Bisbee stage.

"But that'll have to wait for a bit. Got wind of a Mexican smuggler bringin' a mule train through Skeleton Canyon in the next couple of days. Reckon we'd better take care of it first."

9

Skeleton Canyon is a wild, forbidding, overgrown corridor of brush, rocks, and twisting trails that leads from New Mexico into Arizona through the ragged Peloncillo Mountains. It was the common route of the smugglers and other travelers coming and going from Mexico via the San Luis Pass.

It was not strange land to Old Man Clanton and the men

who rode with him that hot July morning. They had been there before, either as highwaymen relieving wayfarers of their valuables, or when passing back and forth from the San Simon to the lush Animas country. And it was a road occasionally traveled rapidly by those seeking sanctuary in the lonely hills and sleepy villages south of the border.

The history of Skeleton Canyon is replete with holdups, participated in by Indians as well as ordinary highwaymen, and the hazards were accepted as part of the price for doing business. It was not a one-sided affair. Americans en route to the larger cities in Mexico's interior were considered fair prey by Mexican outlaws and suffered just as regularly as did the Mexicans journeying into Arizona.

Ringo, well hidden in the brush, watched the slow approach of the smugglers. Elsewhere along the trail were Brocius, the Clantons, and half a dozen more of the Cowboy gang—eleven men in all. It was a lengthy train. There were a large number of sheep, goats, and cattle, as well as pack mules laden with gold, silver, and other valuable items. The leader of the cavalcade, apparently bound for Tucson, had taken every possible precaution. Armed outriders were plentiful and advance scouts, rifles ready, continually probed the brush, the gullies and the canyons, the bulging rock formations.

Ringo rode out the tense moments. This should prove to be a good haul, enough to satisfy Old Man Clanton. Perhaps he would now forget about the deal he had made with Wyatt Earp for Head, Leonard, and Jim Crane. Anger again stirred through Ringo as he thought of the outlaw's duplicity. To sell out a friend—

The hot stillness was shattered by a gun blast. The

signal! Ringo dug spurs into his horse, plunged from the brush into the open. All along the trail other riders were bursting into view, pistols blazing. Ringo, his own weapons out, began to fire. He saw Curly Bill, a dozen paces to his right, crouch low over his saddle, wheel into the midst of the wagon train.

The smugglers, outnumbering the Cowboys three to one, struck back instantly. There was the sudden hammer of gunshots. Dust rose, mixed with the smoke, and the train became a tangled confusion of riders, milling livestock, and overturning vehicles. Ringo rode recklessly back and forth. He had brief glimpses of Old Man Clanton, his white beard streaming in the breeze; of Ike, a gun in each hand, firing with deadly accuracy; of Curly Bill, a wide grin on his face as he dashed in and out of the squealing donkeys, the bleating and bawling livestock.

And then abruptly it was over. The smugglers withdrew, rushing back down the trail for the safety of the dense groves. Old Man Clanton rode in to the center of the train.

"Get roundin' up that stock!" he shouted. "And turn them carts back up so's they'll roll. We got to get out of here!"

Ringo swung in beside Brocius, and with the others, got the train reorganized and finally under way once again. They drove it to a canyon near Galeyville and there divided the spoils. When it was done, Ringo turned to Old Man Clanton.

"Ought to be enough here to make you happy. You can forget that deal you made with Earp."

Clanton grunted, tugged at his beard. "Nope. Ain't never going to get enough to make me happy. I still figure to collect from Earp."

Ringo took a half step forward, felt Curly Bill's hand drop on his shoulder. "Forget it, Johnny," Brocius said.

Ringo hesitated. Old Man Clanton gave him a sly smile and moved off. A short distance away, Ike and Billy Clanton watched with narrow interest, their rifles half raised and ready.

"Not the time," Brocius murmured.

"Maybe," John Ringo replied, "but it's going to come. I'll see to it," he added, and wheeled to his horse.

Reports of the ambush reached Tombstone the day following its occurrence by way of a prospector who had witnessed the affair from a vantage point high up in the canyon. It became the topic of conversation about town and the value of the take was pegged at somewhere near seventy-five thousand dollars. Not a great deal of thought or sympathy was wasted on the Mexicans, however, since they were outlaws and smugglers themselves, but John Clum's *Epitaph* published a letter to Arizona's acting governor, John J. Gosper, which said:

> . . . One of the Cowboys, in relating to me the circumstances [of the ambush], said it was the damndest lot of truck he ever saw. He showed me a piece of bullion; I should judge it to be one half gold. Upon my telling him that trouble would likely arise from this his reply was that it was a smuggling train and they would not dare say much. There were three Mexicans killed in the affray. A notorious Cowboy known as John R. [obviously Johnny Ringo] offers to sell all the mutton the town can consume at one dollar per head. No

secrecy is observed in this kind of transaction.

And no effort was ever made to arrest any of the Cowboys who participated in the raid although almost every person in Tombstone had a fairly accurate idea as to who the twelve men were.

During the time of the raid and the subsequent frivolity that ensued, Harry Head, Bill Leonard, and Jim Crane had remained patiently in hiding at a place near Eureka Springs, New Mexico. Curly Bill's messenger, Indian Charlie, dispatched to warn them of Old Man Clanton's duplicity, had somehow missed them on the trail. Fortunately, however, they tired of waiting and came finally to the conclusion that the projected raid on the Bisbee stage had been canceled.

Turned restless, Crane elected to ride on down into the Animas, where he would be near the Mexican border in the event that trouble, in the shape of Wyatt Earp, developed. There were several ranches in the area and he could work and lie low. Head and Leonard, unwilling to press their luck, struck off into southern New Mexico's Big Hatchet Mountain country.

Poor cards at the gambling tables, and the cost of living high during the two weeks following the ambush of the smuggler train, developed again the need for ready cash among Curly Bill, Old Man Clanton, and several others less expert than Ringo and men of his class. A report reached them of a cattle herd being driven across Sonora and they decided a quick stint at rustling was the solution.

They made the short ride into Mexico, succeeded in capturing the herd, somewhere around three hundred head, and brought it back to the Animas, where they quartered it on Old Man Clanton's ranch. The usual procedure at such times was to graze the stock on the lush pasturage of the Animas briefly, and then move it north to market.

One man was left to guard the stolen herd while Curly Bill and the remaining men drifted on up to his place, where they would while away time drinking and card-playing until it was prudent to sell the cattle.

The Mexicans, still smarting from the affair in Skeleton Canyon, and now further infuriated by this new outrage, gathered in force and struck back. They swept down on the herd, and the lone rider who was guarding it—outnumbered probably twenty or thirty to his one—kept under cover until it was all over and then raced to advise Old Man Clanton and Curly Bill of the loss.

Brocius, informed of the counter raid, sent to Galeyville for all available help. John Ringo, with half a dozen riders, responded at once and the party rode off in pursuit of the Mexicans.

They overtook the slow-moving herd—now totaling considerably more than its original three hundred head, as the *vaqueros* had added a few American beeves to the lot—in San Luis Pass. In the face of a bold attack by the Cowboys, the Mexicans scattered and fled into the hills. The herd was turned and driven back into the Animas Valley and onto Clanton range again.

Old Man Clanton took no more chances with the vengeful Mexicans. With five men to assist him in the handling of the cattle—one of them Jim Crane, for whom he had struck a Judas bargain with Wyatt Earp—he waited only a few days and then started west with the herd. The first evening, under a showering sky, they camped in Guadalupe Canyon, on the Arizona-New Mexico line.

At daybreak, gray and misty, they awoke and prepared to get the cattle into motion. It had been a bad, uncomfortable night, with rain falling intermittently. Clanton and his five men had stuck close to the shelters they had improvised in and beneath the chuck wagon. Only one rider, Harry Earnshaw, had pulled off early to check the bedded cattle.

He had just paused to look back when the crash of rifles filled the canyon and sent the echoes rolling out across the flats. He wheeled quickly, glanced toward the camp. Old Man Clanton was lying face down in the mud. Two others, one Jim Crane, sprawled near the fire they had just built. A fourth man, still in his blankets, also was dead. The rifle fire continued and he saw the last of the crew, a man named Lang, plunging for the shelter of the rocks. Half a dozen bullets smashed into him and he fell.

Earnshaw drew back farther into the brush. He saw a dozen *vaqueros* emerge from the canyon slopes and move downward. They were cautious, still held their weapons ready for instant use as though they half expected the white-bearded old Clanton and his men to rise again and oppose them. But all were dead. Earnshaw, well hidden, waited until the Mexicans had searched the bodies for valuables and started the herd back toward the San Luis Pass. Then he spurred his horse hard for the nearest habitation, the Cloverdale Ranch. He gave an account of the raid to the rancher there, and continued on to Curly Bill's place.

Ringo and Brocius, with several more, after listening to Earnshaw, rode down to Guadalupe Canyon and brought out the bodies. They buried them, side by side, in the Animas Valley—Old Man Clanton, Dick Grey, Bill Lang, Bud Snow, and Jim Crane.

When it was done Ringo turned to Brocius. "What about the herd? Do we go after it?"

Curly Bill shook his head. "Those *vaqueros* got too much of a start on us now. My guess is we'd head straight into an ambush, anyway."

Earnshaw looked thoughtfully at the five graves. "Lucky break for me I rode out for a squint at them critters. I'd be layin' there myself if I hadn't took the notion."

"Three hundred lousy steers," someone else murmured. "Sure ain't worth that many men."

Ringo considered that statement. It was right, of course, but when a man strapped on a gun and drew a mask across his face, he accepted the consequences. Everything had its price—one that must be paid eventually.

"Guess this washes out the deal the Old Man had cooked up with Wyatt," Ringo said.

"Glad of that," Curly Bill said. "Bound to have been trouble if he'd pulled it off."

John Ringo nodded. "I'll guarantee that," he said, and paused. Then, "Guess this makes you the ramrod of the outfit."

Brocius grinned. "Taking over the job might not be as easy as it sounds. Expect Ike's going to feel he ought to step into his pa's boots."

Ringo swung his dark, brooding face to Curly Bill. "Ike better think again. He'll never make it."

10

During this time, Tombstone also had undergone change. A disastrous fire swept the settlement late in June of that year, 1881, and Town Marshal Ben Sippy, unable to control the rioting and halt the looters, resigned. Virgil Earp was appointed to succeed him, and the balance of power in the silent war between John Behan's law-enforcement faction and that of Wyatt Earp swung to the latter. The *Epitaph*, the newspaper that supported Earp, was jubilant; the *Nugget*, which continued to back Behan, never gave up, however, and continued to hammer away despite Earp's gaining the upper hand.

Ike Clanton moved boldly to assume the chieftainship his father, in death, had vacated. He got into immediate touch with Wyatt Earp and advised him of Jim Crane's demise in Guadalupe Canyon. He told the lawman that Bill Leonard and Harry Head reportedly had been seen in the New Mexico town of Hachita, a small settlement east of the Peloncillos. He had sent Joe Hill to verify the information.

Hill returned and brought with him the news that the two men were, indeed, in Hachita—and very dead. Both had been killed in a gunfight with the Haslett brothers, Ike and Bill. Earp dispatched Morgan to learn if Hill's words were true. Morgan quickly verified them. This closed the book on the matter of the men who attempted to rob the Benson stage and killed driver Bud Philpot and passenger Roerig insofar as Wyatt Earp was concerned.

But not for John Ringo.

With Brocius at his side, he halted Hill on Allen Street and ordered him to repeat his report on Head's and Leonard's deaths. When it was finished Ringo whirled to his friend.

"We can thank the Clantons for this! And by God, they're going to answer to me for it!"

"Why the Clantons?" Curly Bill asked, trying to calm the angry Ringo. "They didn't do it."

"They're the ones who started it. If they hadn't made that deal with Earp—"

"Might as well blame him, too," Curly Bill said with a shrug. "I know how you feel, Johnny. Bill and Harry were friends of mine, and I'm for squaring things for them. But let's get the right boys. Let's pay a little call on the Hasletts."

This satisfied the harsh anger that gripped John Ringo and they rode out that night for Hachita. Late the morning of the next day they entered the settlement and pulled up in front of the Hasletts' store. Dismounting, they went inside the shadowy building. Ike and his brother, Bill, were behind the counter.

"You shot down a couple of friends of ours," Ringo said, coming straight to the point. "Got them both in the back."

Bill Haslett said, "Caught them robbing our place. Guess we had a right—"

"It didn't have to be when their backs were turned," Brocius said. "Go for your guns!"

The small building rocked with the blasts of the pistols. When the swirling smoke lifted, Ringo and Brocius still stood in the center of the room. The Hasletts lay dead on the floor.

Ringo turned to Curly Bill. The tension and hard, driving anger were gone from him now. The obligation he felt toward Head and Leonard—and all men he considered his friends—had been discharged.

"That's settled," he said. "Let's go."

They wheeled about and strode to their waiting horses. Mounting, they rode down Hachita's quiet, deserted street, unchallenged by anyone, and returned to Galeyville.

Earp's new-found strength in Tombstone and his entrenched position failed to have any noticeable effects upon the Cowboys. They continued their activities, preying constantly upon cattlemen and waylaying stage coaches whenever they thought there was anything of value aboard. Brocius, to step up the efficiency of the organization whose leadership he was assuming, installed a member of the gang, Pete Spence, in a house directly across the street from the Earp cabin in Tombstone as a means for keeping closer tabs on the lawmen.

On September 8, 1881, the Tombstone-Bisbee coach was held up near the town of Hereford. Around thirty-five hundred dollars were taken from the strongbox and the passengers. The driver, McDaniels, recognized one of the bandits as Pete Spence and another as Frank Stilwell, a deputy of Sheriff Behan's and a known member of the Cowboys.

McDaniels also stated that two more road agents stood off in the brush but he was unable to recognize them. He notified Earp as soon as possible after the holdup occurred and the lawman formed a posse in which were his brother Morgan, and Fred Dodge, and Marshal Williams of the Wells Fargo office. Behan sent along two of his deputies,

Dave Neagle and William Breakenridge.

They picked up the trails of the four horses and followed them into Bisbee. They located Stilwell and arrested him but during this the remaining three robbers disappeared. Earp then sent Stilwell back to Tombstone in the custody of the two Wells Fargo men and, with Morgan, struck out for Charleston after Spence. They succeeded in capturing him and added his presence to that of Stilwell, by then locked in jail in Tombstone.

To prevent Behan from taking charge, Earp swore out federal warrants against the pair and took both to Tucson for a hearing. They were indicted and released on several thousand dollars' bail. Wyatt's clever action so infuriated Ike Clanton that, backed by the McLowry brothers, he cornered Morgan Earp on the street in Tombstone and threatened his life if he or any of the Earps ever pulled such a trick on him. Morgan coolly promised Clanton that should the occasion ever arise when he or any of the Earps could hang a charge that would stick on Ike, or anyone else in the ranks of the Cowboys, they most certainly would do so—and he had damn well better believe it.

This affront to Ike's pride was not taken lightly. It reflected upon his fancied position as new leader of the band, and a few days later, on October twenty-second, with his brother Billy and the two McLowrys, he rode into town prepared to prove himself.

They swaggered up and down Allen Street, visiting all the saloons en route, with Ike sparing no opportunity for making it known to all in earshot that he was captaining the Cowboy element. To further prove his influence he went finally to Sheriff John Behan and secured the release of Billy Claiborne, who was being held for the murder of a man named Hickey. Not satisfied with that display of authority, he returned to the jail and either arranged for the liberation or engineered the escape of four more clan members—Milt Hicks, Jim Sharp, Yank Thompson, and Jesse Harris—all behind bars for rustling and murder.

"Reckon that shows who is ramrod around here," he declared when the word of his actions got around. "Before I'm through people'll are going to know the Clantons still call the shots."

That same afternoon Curly Bill, with Ringo and twenty or more outlaws, including Spence and Stilwell, who gave their allegiance to Brocius, rode in. They stood off to one side listening to Ike and his followers for a time. Then Curly Bill, taking his cue from Ike Clanton, began a demonstration of his force, and for a while the two opposing but friendly factions took over the streets of Tombstone.

It was all a big joke to Brocius and eventually he and his followers tired of the game and scattered, some riding on to Charleston, others settling down in various saloons. But Ike Clanton wasn't finished. He now directed his attention to the Earps, telling all who would listen that a showdown was in the offing, that he intended to drive them from Tombstone, once and for good.

The Safety Committee saw big trouble brewing and proposed to organize enough vigilantes to oust both groups from the settlement. Virgil Earp refused the suggestion but he did deputize Wyatt, Morgan, and Doc Holliday as assistant marshals just in case matters got out of hand. Evening came, however, and tension eased somewhat.

By daylight of the twenty-fifth the Cowboys had pulled out completely. Some, it was reported, had gone to Charleston; others to Galeyville or the Clanton and McLowry ranches. The Safety Committee, and the law, breathed easier. Tombstone lay quiet in the warm, fall sunshine.

And then, abruptly, trouble.

Late in the afternoon Ike Clanton and Tom McLowry rode in. They left their horses at the corral and checked in at the Grand Hotel. Leaving their guns in their room, they began to circulate about town, playing a few hands of poker here and there, spending brief minutes in the saloons, where they bought drinks liberally. It was plainly evident in the actions of the two men that something was afoot. A short time after their arrival word reached Tombstone that Billy Clanton, Frank McLowry, and Billy Claiborne were en route from Charleston, reportedly to join with Ike and Tom.

The Earps considered the information and brushed off the possibility of major violence. John Ringo and Curly Bill weren't with them, they said. And without that pair of expert pistoleers, the affair would likely turn out to be just a repeat of the drunken performance the Clanton clique had exhibited previously.

That night Ike's voluble tongue brought him face to face with Doc Holliday, who eventually suggested that Ike step out into the street and make good his threats. Clanton declined, pointing out that he carried no weapon. Morgan Earp intervened at that moment and persuaded Holliday to overlook the incident and go on to his room.

Patrons of the saloon where the meeting had taken place

buzzed with comment, and Ike, seizing the opportunity to further enhance his importance, hurried off to the Grand Hotel for his gun. Then, with Tom McLowry in tow, he began to walk the streets in search of Holliday, declaring in a voice that could be heard for a considerable distance that he intended to kill the gambler-dentist.

He encountered the Earps a short time later and demanded that Wyatt bring Holliday out for a reckoning. The lawman laughed in his teeth and sent him on his way with the admonition that he was drunk and should go sleep it off before he found himself in real trouble.

At daybreak Ike was still going strong. He stood at the corner of Allen and Fifth Streets, armed with both pistol and rifle, and proclaimed he was going to rid Tombstone of the Earp crowd. Elsewhere in the town Billy Clanton, the McLowrys, and Claiborne were making the rounds of all the saloons in quest of the Earps and Doc Holliday. The showdown was at hand, they said, and the Earps were finished. Fear and tension settled over Tombstone and the streets began to clear. The Safety Committee hurried into emergency session.

Suddenly the situation had turned serious. Wyatt Earp, despite the absence of the two men he knew and respected as deadly killers, Ringo and Curly Bill, decided that the Clantons and the McLowrys, plus Billy Claiborne, were a dangerous threat. He met with Virgil and Morgan, told them the only course open was to run down the noisy bunch, disarm and jail them. He sent his two brothers up Fremont Street and chose Allen for himself. He headed toward the corner where Ike was holding forth. When he reached that intersection, Clanton had disappeared.

Virgil and Morgan came upon him a block away. Ike started to swing his rifle up for a quick shot but Virgil, quick as a cat, stepped in, felled the outlaw with a sharp blow to the head with his pistol. The two lawmen then dragged the senseless Clanton off to the courthouse, where Morgan stood guard over him while Virgil went in search of the judge.

Wyatt, hearing of the incident, hurried to the courtroom, now filling rapidly with townspeople who had witnessed the arrest. After listening to a raving discourse from Ike, again conscious, Wyatt turned about and headed into the street. He ran into Tom McLowry as he passed through the doorway. Words were exchanged, after which Earp slapped McLowry smartly across the face. McLowry reached for his gun and Wyatt dropped him to the ground in the same manner that Virgil had subdued Ike Clanton.

Judge Wallace arrived at that time and, hearing the charges, fined Ike twenty-five dollars for disturbing the peace and set him free. Virgil, weathering a storm of threats from the outlaw, held onto the pistol and rifle he had confiscated and told Clanton he could claim them when he left town.

"Won't be needing them then," Ike said, and stalked off.

He went straight to Spangenberg's Gun Shop, where he outfitted himself with a new pistol and a good supply of ammunition. While he was there, his brother Billy, the McLowrys, and Claiborne joined him. Coming out, there were a few hot words exchanged with Wyatt Earp over Frank McLowry's horse, which had wandered onto the sidewalk, and then all moved off down the street to Dexter's Corral, an establishment in which Sheriff John

Behan owned substantial interest.

Wyatt, with his brothers, retired to Hafford's Saloon, on the corner of Fourth and Allen. The lawman was not convinced, as were many others, that trouble had again blown over. Ike Clanton was pushing hard and Wyatt knew the outlaw could not back down now before his Cowboy followers. He had put on a strong show in his bid to dominate the gang and he could hardly be expected to call it quits at that point. Wyatt was about to express that opinion when a man burst into the saloon.

"Wyatt! You'd better get the vigilantes lined up! Ike's squarin' off for a showdown."

Earp said, "We can handle Ike." He turned to Virgil, sent him over to the Wells Fargo office for a shotgun. When he returned, a second messenger had brought word that the outlaws had moved to the O.K. Corral, and would be waiting there.

A third messenger put in an appearance, a man by the name of Coleman. "Clanton's offering you a deal," he said. "Told me to tell you a shoot-out could be avoided if you'd leave town. All three of you and Doc Holliday. If you won't accept, then he means to fight."

Sheriff Behan, attracted by the gathering crowd, offered his suggestion. "Take him up on it, Earp. Let's don't have wholesale killing around here."

Virgil said, "You know we can't back off now before them, sheriff. How about you and your deputies throwing in with us? Maybe we can avoid a shooting. Enough of us could disarm and arrest them."

Behan shook his head. "Not my job to keep the law inside the town limits."

By this time the whole of Tombstone's population was aware of what was shaping up. Members of the vigilantes and the Safety Committee began to gather in front of Hafford's. They offered to take over for the Earps, and descend upon the Cowboys in such numbers that, by sheer weight, they'd suppress them. It was a good thought but Wyatt Earp realized that in it lay no final answer. Eventually it would have to be settled between the Earps and the Clantons. Also, it would be a mistake for one part of the townspeople to line up openly behind them and thereby oppose that other substantial faction that sympathized with the Cowboys. The result could be trouble of a serious nature.

"Our job," he said, declining the suggestion.

He nodded to Morgan and Virgil and they moved out of Hafford's and started down Fourth Street. Doc Holliday came onto the scene at that moment and joined the march. Virgil handed him the Wells Fargo short-barreled shotgun and the handful of shells he had picked up.

When they reached the intersection of Fourth and Fremont, they swung left, walking four abreast. Sheriff Behan interrupted their progress briefly in front of Bauer's Meat Market but they waved him off, and he ducked inside a photographer's shop. The Earp party wheeled into the corral, reached from the street by a corridor-like driveway. They came to a halt. All Tombstone paused, waited in breathless silence. Then Virgil Earp's voice broke across the tense hush.

"You men are under arrest! Throw up your hands!"

Seconds later the hills echoed with the rattle of gunshots.

11

The two men who might have written a different ending to the fight at the O.K. Corral that morning of October 26, 1881—John Ringo and Curly Bill Brocius—were in Galeyville at the time it transpired. Old heads at the game of outlawry, they were observing that well-turned adage never to push a lawman into a corner where he would be forced to act—or lose the confidence of his public. A man followed that rule if he expected to continue operations in the same vicinity.

And the Tombstone area was a vault of riches for them in many ways. Not only was it fat pickings but their activities, if not too flagrant, were more or less ignored by Sheriff John Behan and his deputies. All they needed to do in return was support him politically. The Earp faction had been the only blemish on the plum—and that not too serious. But Ike Clanton, in his need to prove himself, had compelled the Earps to act. It could mean a great deal of trouble.

Curly Bill was considerably disturbed when he heard of the affair. "If they'd killed off the Earps, it would have been all right," he said after listening to a report of the shoot-out. One of the crew had ridden up from Tombstone with the news. "What he's done now is stir up a nest of yellow jackets!"

"Ike's raving like a crazy man. He got Behan to charge the Earps and Holliday with murder. Then the grand jury turned it down."

"Naturally would," Ringo said. "Behan could never

make a thing like that stick. How bad did the Earps get shot up?"

"Hardly any. Virgil took a bullet in the leg. Morgan was hit in the shoulder. Nobody else got more'n a scratch."

"Where's Ike and Claiborne now?"

"Both got locked up for a spell, then Behan turned them loose. Took them over to Harry Woods at the *Nugget* and they gave him a big story about the killings. Reckon the sheriff's out to get people on his side. Woods' story says the Earps' killing Billy Clanton and the McLowry boys was plain murder."

"Be a few swallow that, not many," Curly Bill said. "I figure we'd better go after it in a different way. When's the funeral?"

"Sunday."

"Good. Here's what we do. I don't give a hang about Ike, but we're not about to let the Earps think they've got us buffaloed. We ride in Saturday. Roust out everybody so there'll be plenty there at that funeral. I aim to make this a show nobody's going to forget."

On that Saturday afternoon, Sheriff Behan, with the still furious Ike Clanton swearing vengeance and ignoring the grand jury, went before a Tombstone judge and swore out warrants for the three Earps and Doc Holliday. He charged them with the murder of Billy Clanton and Tom and Frank McLowry. After considerable wrangling the bail was finally set at ten thousand dollars, with a hearing scheduled for the following Monday.

All that night Brocius and Ringo, supported by the rest of the Cowboys, paraded around Tombstone making it clear they had no fear of the Earps and announcing they backed Sheriff John Behan, and Ike Clanton, to the limit in their desire to prosecute the "lawless killers."

On Sunday the funeral of the three men was held and an estimated two hundred mourners marched through Tombstone in solemn procession—better than half that number being residents of the town who felt the Cowboys were getting a raw deal from the Earps.

On Monday the hearing began as prescribed, with one exception—the judge refused to admit anyone to the courtroom except court officials and those actually involved in the shoot-out. Thus Ringo and Brocius, along with others, were not permitted to be present.

"No use us hanging around here," Brocius said after the judge's ruling became known. "We'll keep a few of the boys on the streets, just for looks. Rest of us might as well go on about our business."

So it remained while the hearing dragged on with charge and countercharge, accusations and denials winging back and forth, all of which were faithfully revealed to the public from two wholly different and opposed angles by the *Nugget* and the *Epitaph.*

On December 1, 1881, the judge rendered his decision. The charges against Wyatt Earp and Doc Holliday were dropped, and both were exonerated. The warrants pending for Morgan and Virgil, still bedridden with their wounds, were quashed.

Ike Clanton's rage was fearful. "They ain't getting away with this!" he shouted when the decision was handed down. "It's a fixed-up job. The Earps had everything cut and dried with that judge. I'm going to make my own verdict!"

John Ringo, lounging with others in Barton's Saloon in Charleston, glanced at Clanton and smiled dryly. "How?"

"Taking things in my own hands, that's how! I'll get the Earps, every last one of them! And Doc Holliday, too. And there's a few more—that editor at the *Epitaph*, Clum, and the judge, and those Wells Fargo agents. I'm making me up a list and I'm going to get them one by one."

Brocius, sitting at a table a few paces away, said, "You'll do it on your own, then. Don't expect any of us to side you. Was a damn fool thing you started, anyway."

Clanton stared at Curly Bill for a long minute. Finally he shrugged. "Don't worry none about that. I'll take care of it. But I expect there's some around who feel like I do about the Earps."

On December fourteenth, Clanton, with several of the gang, intercepted and halted the stage carrying John Clum, recently elected to the office of mayor, to Benson. Clum intended to take the train East for a visit with his young son. The holdup, or actually assassination attempt, since the coach carried no money or bullion, was badly bungled by Clanton and the mayor escaped on foot into the darkness.

During the confusion the horses bolted and the stage eluded the outlaws and reached the small settlement of Contention. There the mayor was found to be missing and frantic telegrams were sent to Sheriff Behan in Tombstone, who had jurisdiction in this particular instance. The worst was feared for Clum. The entire town had been in a state of nervous apprehension over the "list" Ike Clanton was supposed to have prepared, and the mayor was known to be one of those most prominent.

Clum, during all the excitement over his disappearance and while Behan with a small posse rushed to the scene of the attempted abduction, found his way through the night to one of a mining company's stamping mills. There he rested for a brief time and then, borrowing a horse, rode on to Benson, passing almost through a group of sleeping men who had pulled off the road and who, he was certain, were part of the gang sent to abduct him.

Behan, at the point where the coach had been halted, found signs of the outlaws' presence and discovered a large amount of spilled blood, which subsequently proved to be that of one of the stagecoach horses accidentally shot in the melee. He turned up nothing else that would lead to the whereabouts of Clum or his assailants, and so gave it up until daylight.

The mayor's arrival in Benson cleared up the matter and when word was relayed to Tombstone, members of the Safety Committee and the law-abiding citizens breathed easier. At first report, all thought the Cowboys had made good their threats of revenge and the town had pitched into a turmoil of jitters. All those who had been involved on the side of the Earps had prepared themselves for the worst. Some even suggested wiring Prescott for military protection.

And the thought was still being bandied about. The very fact that an attempt had been made on Clum's life was proof enough the outlaws meant business. Earp and his followers girded themselves for more trouble.

It came quickly in the person of John Ringo.

12

Wyatt Earp, at the insistence of friends and the Safety Committee, had moved his injured brothers from the family cabin off Fremont Street to the second floor of the Cosmopolitan Hotel. There they could be more easily guarded. He was provided with an adjoining room and Doc Holliday took up quarters directly across the hall.

Almost exactly opposite on Allen Street stood another hostelry, the Grand. There the Brocius-Clanton crowd usually stayed when in town for any length of time. On this particular cold December day John Ringo, wearing the huge bearskin coat that was all too familiar in Tombstone, came from the Grand and halted on the sidewalk. There was a hard set to his jaw and the glint in his eyes mirrored the anger that stirred him. Two men strolling by glanced at him, spoke, and then quickened their step. Ringo on the prod was a man you left to himself.

He was looking for Doc Holliday. Three times in as many days reports had reached him concerning the gunman-gambler. Doc was talking about him, saying all manner of disparaging and insulting things. The last occasion, according to Ike Clanton, who had been present, was the previous night in the Oriental Saloon. Ringo had listened to Clanton's recital of the incident, decided the moment had arrived to do something about it.

He stood there on the walk for several minutes, a big man who looked even larger in the coat he wore. Holliday, following habit, should be appearing. He would come from the Oriental, cross Fifth, and saunter up Allen on the opposite side en route to the Cosmopolitan. There was movement behind Ringo in the doorway of the Grand but he did not look around as Ike Clanton and several more of the Cowboy clan eased into the open and took up positions along the front of the building.

"Here he comes," someone murmured in a tight, expectant voice.

Ringo watched Holliday pause at the corner, draw a cigar from a silver case, and thrust it between his teeth. The gambler struck a match with his thumbnail, held it to the tip of the weed, and inhaled. Blowing the smoke out in a long sigh, he continued on. Ringo crossed the street and halted near the entrance to the hotel. He waited until Holliday was directly before him.

"Far enough, Doc. I want to talk to you."

Holliday came to a slow stop. He removed the cigar from his mouth. "All right, Ringo. Let's hear it."

Magically a crowd began to gather, standing back at a respectful distance. As if by prearrangement those who backed Ringo grouped on one side of Allen, those who sided with Holliday on the other.

"Understand you've been talking about me when I'm not around. Let's hear you say it to my face."

Holliday dropped his cigar to the dust. "Doubt if you're sober enough to understand it," he said, his words blunt and clear, "but here it is! I said most first-class horse thieves like you won't usually stoop to bushwhacking like a few cutthroats I could name."

There was a dead silence. Ringo's hands, thrust deep into his pockets, held a pistol in each. Holliday's fancy nickel-plated weapon was visible beneath his coat.

"Could say the same for you," Ringo replied evenly. "First-class gambling man like you licking the boots of back-shooters like the Earps—"

"Good men," Holliday said. "And before this is done with they'll have you and your whole pack either run out of the country or planted on Boot Hill."

"Not the Earps. Take more than them. Wyatt backed off before and I expect he'll do it again if we ever come up to the mark for a showdown."

"Didn't see him backing down at the O.K. Corral—"

"Little different there. Ike's no gun-slinger. Neither was Billy Clanton. Way I see it, it was the McLowrys against all of you. Four to two. Pretty tough odds."

"They picked it," Holliday said. "Was their party. Sorry you weren't there."

"I'm here now, Doc. And I want a retraction of the things you've been saying about me. Make it loud and clear so every man around can hear you."

Holliday studied Ringo's taut face. A half smile pulled at his thin lips. "No. Not here now, not anywhere, Johnny. I let it stand."

"Fine," Ringo said softly. "Was hoping you'd feel that way about it."

Holliday lifted his glance, let it sweep briefly over the crowd. "This is between us, Ringo. Move out into the middle of the street. No use anybody else getting hurt."

Holliday wheeled about, deliberately placed his back to Ringo, and stalked off into the center of Allen. Ringo took one long step after him, felt powerful arms encircle his body, pin his hands to his sides.

"What the hell—"

"There'll be no shooting, not here in town." Flynn, a special deputy appointed by Virgil Earp to fill in, while he was off duty, had come up from behind Ringo.

Doc Holliday, pivoting at the words, shook his head at the lawman. "Turn him loose, Flynn. We're going to settle this right now."

Flynn said, "No," in a stubborn, unyielding voice. "Far as the pair of you are concerned, I reckon it would make no difference to me or anybody else. But was you to open up, we'd have a regular war right quick, judging from the looks of that crowd."

It was true. The gathering, in two distinct camps, were eying each other distrustfully. It would take only the crash of Ringo and Holliday's guns to light a fuse that could end in a massacre.

"Let me go," Ringo said, twisting in the deputy's grasp. "We'll move out to the edge of town. That ought to satisfy you."

Wyatt Earp, hastily summoned by someone, came through the doorway of the Cosmopolitan. He looked about quickly, then walked to where Holliday, poised and waiting, stood.

"Forget it, Doc," he said. "You'd not have a chance. Even if you got Ringo I expect there's half a dozen rifles pointed at you from that room on the second floor of the Grand. They'd drop you in your tracks."

Earp turned to Flynn. "Take Ringo and hand him over to the sheriff. Charge him with carrying weapons. Rest of you people clear off the street. Get moving now—this thing is all over."

Ringo, with Flynn's gun jammed into his spine, marched

to Behan's office. The sheriff, busy at his desk, glanced up. Deputy Breakenridge was in another part of the jail.

"What's the trouble?" Behan asked.

Flynn said, "Carrying firearms and trying to start a ruckus with Doc Holliday. Earp said to hand him over to you."

"To me?" the sheriff echoed, surprised. "I'm not the town marshal. You sure that's what he said?"

"I'm sure."

Behan shrugged. "All right, Flynn. I'll take care of it."

The deputy spun and left the office. Behan looked up at the tall Ringo. "You heard the charge, Johnny. I can't arrest you but maybe you'd better pass me your weapons and stick around inside here until things quiet down a bit."

Ringo obediently handed over his two ivory-handled Colts. Behan slid them into the top drawer of his desk.

"Coffee on the stove there," he said. "Help yourself. Got some errands to run."

Ringo watched Behan move for the door. "What about me? It all right if I arrange bail so I can leave?"

The sheriff paused. "What was it Flynn said you did? Had yourself a fight with Holliday?"

"Never got down to that. Just about ready to settle things when that deputy grabbed me. Wyatt stepped in then and broke it up. Sent me over here with Flynn."

Behan thumbed the sheaf of papers he held in thoughtful silence. Then, "Sure can't arrest a man for arguing on the street—even if I had the jurisdiction. This is a matter for the town marshal but I guess he doesn't want any part of it. Tell you what you do—just leave off your guns for a bit and we'll forget it."

The sheriff opened the door and walked on into the street. Ringo swore. He glanced at Breakenridge.

"How about some coffee?" the deputy suggested.

Ringo shook his head. He could use a drink at that moment but coffee was farthest from his needs. "Don't know what the sheriff's up to but he's sure setting me up like a duck on a pond, taking my guns. I walk out there without them, I'm a dead man."

Breakenridge stepped to Behan's desk. He pulled open the top drawer, into which Ringo's weapons had been dropped.

"You want my opinion," he said, winking slyly, "I don't think he meant it that way. Now, I got to run over to the gunsmith's. While I'm gone you feel free to do just as you please."

Breakenridge left. Ringo lifted the two pistols from the drawer and returned them to his holsters. Five minutes later he was back in the Alhambra Saloon, where the story of his encounter with Doc Holliday was already building into legend.

13

On the heels of the Ringo-Holliday clash, United States Senator George Hearst arrived in Tombstone with the purpose in mind of investing heavily in the area. A rumor sprang up immediately that the Brocius Cowboys had made elaborate plans to kidnap the distinguished visitor and hold him for a large ransom.

The town's important citizens, shocked by the report but turned wary by experience, never doubted the rumor for an instant. They quickly assigned Wyatt Earp to the position of bodyguard and constant companion to Hearst while he was in Cochise County. No attempt was made to abduct the illustrious capitalist and he finally departed after making it known he had decided against any investments. Likely he was the first person to realize Tombstone was on the decline, treasure-wise.

With the senator safely out of the country, Wyatt Earp returned to the settlement and resumed his usual chores. Then, on the night of December twenty-eighth, the outlaws again laid down their challenge.

Virgil, recovered from the wound sustained at the O.K. Corral affair, was back on the job as town marshal. He was making his rounds, and just as he passed the Eagle Brewery, on the corner of Fifth and Allen, the night ripped apart with the blasts of several shotguns. A hail of buckshot hammered into the wall and windows behind the lawman, and a sizable amount of it drove into Virgil's side and arm.

He managed to stay on his feet and saw five men dart out of the shadows of a building under construction on the opposite side of the street. He had no time to throw an answering fire but managed somehow to stagger to the Oriental Saloon, where he knew Wyatt to be at that moment.

Wyatt got his brother to the town's best physician, George Goodfellow, who told the lawman that Virgil's wounds were serious and that his chances were none too promising. Wyatt then hurried off to see if he could learn more concerning the identity of the ambushers. In the building from which the shots had been fired he found Ike

Clanton's hat. Checking farther along the street he located a man who claimed to have seen the killers—or at least three of them.

"Ike Clanton, Frank Stilwell, and Hank Swilling," he said. "That's who they were. Seen them go running by after the shootin'. Every blasted one of them was carryin' a shotgun."

Grim with anger, Wyatt kept on. Virgil had said five men; that was only three. Another witness turned up. He had noticed two men rushing off toward the north end of town. One he did not recognize because of the darkness. He was positive about the second. It was John Ringo, he said.

Earp went straight to the Safety Committee. In a body they called upon Sheriff Behan, demanded he hunt down the would-be assassins and bring them to justice. Behan agreed, went through the motions, and accomplished nothing. There was no real evidence, he pointed out. None that would stand up in court. Only vague reports of certain men having been seen in the dark, running. Maybe they carried guns, maybe they did not. There was nothing conclusive or tangible to go on.

Earp was furious—and worried. He could see the shadow of things to come. The shoot-out at the O.K. Corral had been no solution, no answer to the Cowboy-outlaw element. It had merely heightened the tension and whetted the gang to bolder, more reckless activity. And it had turned Ike Clanton into a skulking savage who sought only bloody revenge for the death of his brother, Billy. A more terrible showdown was now in the wind and this time, against men such as John Ringo, Curly Bill, Pony

Deal, and certain others, the outcome could be much different. They would do their talking with six-guns and not, as Ike Clanton did, with a loud mouth.

The Tombstone Safety Committee, and the Law and Order Party, along with other such organizations, realized the relentless approach of a serious crisis as fully as did Earp. Their solution was to stop John Behan cold at the coming local election slated for January third. The sheriff, and the newspaper that backed him, the *Nugget*, had a ticket of their own choosing in the field and were set to take over the town government—most particularly the job of marshal since Virgil Earp, still in bad shape from the ambush, was out of the running.

The law enforcement faction reasoned that if they could crush Behan at the polls with a group of candidates they knew to be honest, dependable men, they would be taking a long step toward cleaning up the lawless element. The man they chose to run for town marshal was Dave Neagle, one-time deputy of Behan's who presumably broke with the sheriff over the favoritism the lawman showed Ringo and other members of the Cowboys. Their nominee for mayor was John Carr.

On election day both parties had armed guards at the voting booths. Carr and Neagle won by healthy majorities. This was considered an overwhelming mandate for the law-and-order groups, and emboldened, they swore out warrants for the three men thought to have had a part in the assassination attempt on Virgil Earp—Ike Clanton, Frank Stilwell, and Hank Swilling. No warrant was issued for John Ringo, which puzzled a vast number of Tombstone's citizens and aroused considerable speculation.

The accused men surrendered promptly to John Behan. And almost as promptly they produced witnesses who swore the trio could not possibly have been involved in the shooting since they knew them to have been miles away at the time of the incident. As for Clanton's hat, found by Earp in the skeleton of the new building, Ike claimed to have lost it in the hills months previous. He had no idea, of course, who could have found it.

And so all three were set free.

When the hearing was over they joined John Ringo at Hafford's Saloon. He greeted them silently, waved to the bartender to bring drinks for all. After they had settled at his table, Clanton leaned back in his chair.

"Reckon we've showed Earp who's running this town," he said. "He'll think twice before he makes a grab for us again."

Ringo shook his head. "Don't bet on it, Ike. Wyatt won't give up. You three would be smart to take it easy for a week or two, and let things cool down."

Clanton said, "Hell, no!" in a quick sort of way. "I figure we got to do something—prove he don't scare us none."

"Johnny could be right," Swilling said, toying with his drink. "Maybe we ought to hole up for a spell."

"I'm with Ike," Stilwell said. "And to my way of thinking, we ought to pull a couple of jobs just to rub it in."

Ringo shrugged, stared at his long, tapering fingers. He could use some money. His luck at cards had not been good lately, but he had a feeling that it was the wrong time to make such a move as Clanton proposed. Earp would not take his defeat lightly. He would be angry, and ready to act at the first provocation. And this time he would make sure there would be no slip-ups.

"Suit yourself," he said finally. "I'm heading back to Galeyville. If you're smart you'll do the same."

"I'm with you," Swilling said. "The sooner I get out of this town the better I'll like it. What about you boys," he added, raising his glance to Clanton and Stilwell.

"We're going south," Ike replied. "That Bisbee stage ain't been tapped lately. It ought to be ripe."

"You stopping at Charleston and telling Curly Bill about it?" Ringo asked.

Clanton got to his feet. "Maybe," he said. "I'll be deciding that later."

"Tell him," Ringo said bluntly, and shoved back his chair. The four men separated, Ringo and Swilling riding east toward the Chiricahuas, Clanton and Stilwell taking the road for Charleston. They apparently met and convinced Brocius of the merits of their thinking, for on January sixth, two days later, in the Mule Mountains, the stage for Tombstone was held up by five bandits. An $8,500 payroll consigned to the Copper Queen Mine was taken.

During the holdup the driver, Bill Waite, and the guard, Charlie Bartholomew, recognized the robbers to be Curly Bill, Pony Deal, Ike Clanton, Frank Stilwell, and Pete Spence. Word was flashed to Wyatt Earp and he hurriedly took to the road with a posse.

He had scarcely reached the scene of the crime when news of another robbery reached him. Curly Bill and Pony Deal had halted and stripped a second stagecoach, this time near Contention. They had taken $2,500 and made no bones about their identity, even to the point of spurning masks.

Earp wheeled about and started for Contention at a hard run. At last he had Brocius, the leader of the Cowboys, dead to rights. And this time he would nail his hide to the wall. Since the United States mail had been involved in the robberies, it was a federal matter and that fell properly in his jurisdiction. He would capture Curly Bill, rush him off to Tucson for hearing—and thereby remove him from John Behan's kindly ministrations.

There was only one thing that disturbed him—John Ringo had not been reported a member of either party. And generally, where you found Curly Bill, you found Ringo. Could it be there had been a split in the outlaw ranks?

14

Johnny Ringo was having problems of his own.

In Galeyville at the time Curly Bill and the others were relieving the stages of their money shipments, he was being arrested for the robbery of a saloon and gambling hall. Morose and angry, he rode in silence back to Tombstone with the deputy and there reported to John Behan.

"Little thing like this," he said to the sheriff, "didn't call for sending a man after me. If you'd sent word, I would have come in."

Behan nodded. "I know that, but we've got a grand jury indictment on our hands. Looks better this way."

"Don't much like the idea of a deputy showing up and arresting me. Made a hell of a looking thing." It was evident Ringo had suffered considerable embarrassment in the presence of his friends. "I'm telling you straight, John, had it been anybody but one of your boys, he'd be a dead duck right now!"

"Know that, too," Behan said in a placating voice. "I figured you'd be smart enough to realize I had to do it that way. Hear about Curly?"

Ringo said, "No. What happened?"

"Charlie Bartholomew and Bill Waite claim he and four others held up their stage near Bisbee. Got over eight thousand dollars. Then Curly Bill and Pony Deal turn around and hit another coach outside Contention. Took another twenty-five hundred."

"Who were the other three men on the Bisbee job?" Ringo asked.

"Ike Clanton, Pete Spence, and Stilwell."

Ringo was silent. Clanton evidently had stopped to see Brocius; moreover, he had convinced him to take a hand in the raid. Ringo swore softly. Curly Bill should have had more sense.

"There any doubt about the identifications."

"None," Behan replied.

"You going after them?"

"Earp's already down there. Got Sherm McMasters and three, four men with him. Guess he was all cocked and primed for the boys."

"Curly can take care of himself."

"Maybe so," the sheriff said, "but Wyatt's out to get them this time, especially Curly Bill. For once he's got positive identifications and reliable witnesses. Never had that before."

Ringo leaned up against Behan's desk, glanced toward the window. It had been as he had feared. Clanton had played straight into Wyatt Earp's hands. And he had sucked Brocius, Deal, and Pete Spence into it also. But they were old hands at the game. They would make out all right.

"Little matter of catching them first," he murmured. "What about this trouble of mine? Ought to see if I can help Curly—and I can't do that if I'm cooped up here."

The door swung open and a man rushed in. "Sheriff! Jackson's wanting to know if you're riding to Charleston with him and the vigilantes he's getting together. He thinks somebody from your office should go along."

"To Charleston? What for?"

"Earp's sent word he's got Curly Bill and Pony Deal cornered there. Wants some help so's he can take both of them. That's why he's got the vigilantes together."

Ringo listened with rising alarm. Most of the Cowboys were in Galeyville, or scattered elsewhere at that time. There would be few, if any, in Charleston. Wyatt Earp, backed by a dozen heavily armed men, would have little problem taking Brocius and Deal.

Behan said, "Tell Jackson to go on ahead. I'll send one of my deputies, or come myself, soon as I can."

The man wheeled and hurried from the office. Ringo followed him to the door. He paused there.

"Got a little business to attend to, sheriff. Expect you'll have to excuse me for a couple of hours."

Behan grinned. "All right, Johnny. Just you be sure you're back here in time to appear before Judge Stillwell."

Ringo hurried to his horse, mounted, and started for Charleston. A few miles below Tombstone he caught sight of the vigilante party. He swung wide, passed them without being noticed. He forded the San Pedro River above the bridge, guessing that Earp and his men would be waiting somewhere near that point, and entered the settlement at its northern end. He found Curly Bill and Deal resting in Barton's Saloon.

"Get out of here," he said, wasting no time. "And make it fast. Earp's moving in, set on taking you both."

Brocius and Deal came to their feet. Curly Bill said, "Might be a good time to have it out with him."

"Not much it wouldn't," Ringo replied. "He's got a dozen or more vigilantes with him. Any of our boys in town?"

"Only a couple, maybe three."

"Wouldn't stand a chance," Ringo said. "Best thing is for you two to pull out. Doubt if they're over ten minutes behind me."

Pony Deal said, "You're not coming along?"

"No, I'll wait here, stall them off to give you as much time as possible. Got to get back to Tombstone, anyway."

Brocius and Deal left at once. Ringo located two of the gang in a back room of Ayers' place and drafted them into service. With rifles, they moved out into the center of Charleston's one street and there awaited the arrival of Wyatt Earp and the vigilantes.

The lawmen were not long in coming. Curly Bill and Pony Deal could have gotten no farther than a half mile from the town's limits when Wyatt and the vigilantes appeared, riding slowly and warily down the narrow roadway. Earp saw Ringo and his two companions, lifted his hand signaling a halt. He pushed on ahead a dozen paces. He studied the tall outlaw closely.

Then he said, "I want no trouble with you, Ringo. I'm

looking for Curly Bill and Pony Deal."

"You won't find them here."

"They're around," Earp said. "I intend to find them."

"You calling me a liar, Wyatt?" Ringo asked softly.

There was a long, tight silence. One of the vigilantes coughed, cleared his throat. Earp said, finally, "I know Brocius and Pony rode in here a short while ago. And I'm pretty sure they're still around."

"You're wrong. They're not—and you can believe that."

Earp again was quiet. Then, "How long you been here?"

"Long enough."

The lawman half turned, threw his glance to the waiting vigilantes. "Anybody pass you on the road coming from Tombstone?"

Someone in the posse said, "Nope. Sure wasn't."

"You hear anybody—maybe off the road?"

A voice said, "Come to think of it, I did. Heard a horse over to the right of us, toward the river. Didn't give it no thought—and I didn't see nobody."

A long sigh slipped from Wyatt Earp's lips. He squared himself around in his saddle. "Guess that explains it. Ringo, I ought to arrest you for interfering with the law, but I don't think it would do any good."

"You mean it was him I heard along the river?" the vigilante member asked.

"Pretty evident, isn't it? He heard we were moving in on Curly Bill and Deal and rode ahead to warn them."

Ringo said nothing, thereby neither affirming nor disagreeing with the lawman's conclusion.

"You can take another message to them," Earp said, directing his words to Ringo. "Tell them I've got a case against them this time and I won't quit until I've got them both locked behind bars."

Ringo shrugged. "Never had much experience running messages," he said dryly. "Can't seem to get them straight. Why don't you just come ahead and look around town? You might run into them after all. Then you could tell them yourself."

"Don't figure there's much chance of that," Earp said, "but maybe I will. Might be a good idea if you came along, too."

Ringo smiled faintly. "Much obliged, but I've got to be getting back to Tombstone. Judge Stillwell is expecting me. So long, marshal. See you again sometime," he added, and turned to his horse.

15

The continual flow of reports to the capital at Prescott regarding the lawless activities of the Brocius-Clanton band, the complaints of mine owners and probably the lamentations of the Wells Fargo people, who, despite an enviable record elsewhere for protecting their passengers and cargoes, had failed consistently in Cochise County, finally got action from the higher echelons of the territorial government.

In January, 1882, Acting Governor John J. Gosper and United States Marshal C. P. Dake rode into Tombstone. They immediately went into closed-door sessions with the merchants, mine owners, law officials, and other influential citizens. When it was done with, Wyatt Earp emerged with enforcement powers that placed him only one step below Dake insofar as authority was concerned and that made Sheriff John Behan technically his subordinate.

They appointed Morgan and Virgil Earp, Doc Holliday, and half a dozen others to serve as federal deputies, and granted Wyatt the privilege of adding more when and if he felt it necessary.

They issued to him one order only—clean up Cochise County. To further prosecute that end, the government deposited five thousand dollars to his account in the bank for expenses. The citizens of Tombstone immediately subscribed another five thousand and then Wells Fargo, in conjunction with the Southern Pacific Railway, not to be outdone, matched that with still another five thousand dollars.

Judge Stillwell capped the proposed drive by issuing a handful of warrants, blank and otherwise, to cover all outlaws in the county, and offered the succinct advice that it probably was wise not to be too diligent in bringing in prisoners; that lying dead in the mesquite they could cook up no alibis.

John Carr, Tombstone's mayor, brought forth a proclamation calling upon all citizens in Cochise County to aid Wyatt in the pursuit of his duties, and the big cleanup was then officially underway.

The lawman and his associates went to work energetically. They began to scout the country, arresting and sending back to Tombstone many of the lesser fry of the Brocius-Clanton Cowboys, driving others from the territory entirely. But the dragnet failed to turn up anyone of importance.

In February, John Behan, smarting in his inferior role,

appeared in Contention with Ike Clanton and swore out murder warrants for the Earps and Holliday, thus reopening the O.K. Corral incident. Whether it was only an effort to slow down Earp's campaign by discrediting him in the eyes of Prescott officials, or simply a continuation of the burning hatred and desire for revenge that seethed within Ike Clanton, is not known.

Earp notified Behan not to bother serving the warrants, that he, with Morgan and Holliday, would present themselves before the justice of the peace in Contention on the designated date. Virgil, however, was still disabled by his wounds and could not appear. The sheriff was given stern warning not to disturb him.

Behan accepted the terms and on February fourteenth, Wyatt, with Morgan and Holliday, surrendered to Behan at his office. They refused to give up their weapons, however, and declined also to ride in the buckboard the sheriff had provided.

"You're not herding us down the road where your friends can shoot us in the back," Wyatt told Behan. "We stay on our saddles."

Behan was reinforced by his undersheriff, Harry Woods of the *Nugget*, Deputy William Breakenridge—and Special Deputy Ike Clanton. For a brief time the promise of violence hung heavily in the cold, crisp air of Tombstone, and then at the critical moment a posse of fully armed vigilantes, led by attorney Colonel William Herring, appeared on the scene. They made it plain they were going along to see that the accused men received a fair and bloodless hearing.

The group proceeded to Contention, where it was

quickly shown by Herring that the justice was far beyond his depth and had not the slightest jurisdiction in the case. The judge immediately transferred the matter to the courts in Tombstone. The party trooped back there, went before the bench, and the warrants were quashed. John Behan once again was defeated in his efforts to oust the Earps, and Ike Clanton's revenge continued to go unsatisfied.

Wyatt and his deputies resumed their campaign to destroy the outlaw kingdom. The Cattleman's Association, taking courage from the rigid, determined attitude of the firmed-up law, threw off their shackles of fear. They lynched a few minor rustlers they caught red-handed, and came up with a one-thousand-dollar reward for Curly Bill Brocius, dead or alive.

Ike Clanton, visualizing a quick profit, killed a luckless Mexican and carried his head in a sack to the president of the organization, Henry C. Hooker. He claimed it to be that of Curly Bill and demanded the reward. He was laughed off the premises by Hooker and others who knew Brocius only too well.

As could be expected, Earp's drive eventually netted some of the larger fish. He captured Frank Stilwell and Pete Spence. Taken into Tombstone, they made bond and agreed to appear before a grand jury in Tucson on March twenty-first.

Shortly before that date the pair was joined in town by Hank Swilling and the half-breed known as Indian Charlie. Earp, in Tombstone at the time, was tipped off that Stilwell and others were scheming to kill him, along with his brothers Virgil and Morgan, and Doc Holliday. It was to be some time that night, his informant said; just how and exactly where it was not known.

Wyatt and Morgan went immediately to the hotel, where Virgil, still incapacitated, lived. They arranged for an around-the-clock guard for him and then turned their efforts to hunting down Stilwell and Spence, and the two who had recently joined them, Swilling and Indian Charlie. They spent the entire afternoon combing Tombstone but when darkness came, they had found none of them and gave it up. Apparently it had been a false rumor.

That night they attended a stage show at Schieffelin Hall, after which Wyatt went on to his hotel room to retire. Morgan, not ready for sleep, dropped by Hatch's Billiard Parlor on Allen Street for a late game.

A short time later Wyatt Earp, now finding himself fully awake and strangely disturbed, dressed and walked to Hatch's. The rumor of the intended assassination had appeared to be no more than that—rumor. But somehow Wyatt could not quell the uneasiness that filled his mind.

16

At the time Governor Gosper and Federal Marshal Dake were in Tombstone investing Wyatt Earp with super powers in law enforcement, John Ringo, Curly Bill Brocius, and a fair number of their followers were in Galeyville taking it easy. The weather in the Arizona hills had been sharp and not suitable to riding. Cash at the moment was plentiful among the outlaws and the main diversion was poker and a well-liquored hot-stove league holding forth in the various saloons.

Ringo, in a poker game with Russian Bill, Pony Deal,

Billy Claiborne, and two others, had been winning consistently. Elsewhere in the saloon Curly Bill slept, slouched deep in a chair, hat pulled low over his eyes. The room was thick with tobacco smoke and lamps had been lighted to offset the grayness of the day outside.

"Where's Ike?" Ringo asked. "Haven't noticed him around since yesterday morning."

"Went to Tombstone," Pony Deal replied. "Said he had to see Behan about something."

"He still after the sheriff to push a murder charge against the Earp crowd for killing Billy and the McLowrys?"

Claiborne said, "He'll never give it up. Way he hates Wyatt and Holliday is something fierce. Told me he was going to get them for it if it's the last thing he ever does."

"Probably will be," Ringo said dryly, laying down his winning cards. "Think I'll ride into town myself. Getting tired of this place."

Russian Bill, a comparative newcomer to the band, leaned back in his chair. "I'm tired of the whole country. I'm going on into New Mexico—or maybe Texas. How about coming along?"

Ringo shook his head. "Arizona suits me. Had my fill of Texas and I sure never lost anything in New Mexico."

"Maybe we all ought to be thinking about pulling out," Pony Deal said, rolling a cigarette. "Pickings are getting a little slim. Some of the mines are about done for. There ain't none of them shipping bullion like they used to."

Ringo shrugged. "Always a chance to pick up some money, even if the mines cut down. They're still handling payrolls by stage mail."

"With Earp and his deputies out prowling the country,

makes it some tougher. What about him?"

"Wyatt? He'll be moving on soon. He'll get fed up when the town cools off and the excitement dies down. Same goes for Holliday."

"You hear that Wyatt sold out his interest in the Oriental?"

"Good sign," Ringo said. "Shows he's about ready to drift."

Claiborne, twirling a tumbler half filled with whiskey between his fingers, said, "How's it happen you and Wyatt never tangled good, Johnny? Always looked like bad blood between you and I've been expecting something to pop. Only it never did."

There was an immediate hush in the room. Outside, the winter wind tore at the wooden structure, slamming the loose boards, rattling the windows. Claiborne was treading on dangerous ground and all knew it. Ringo was no man to get personal with. He talked little, kept his thoughts to himself, and never mentioned the past. Only one man alive was considered close to him—Curly Bill.

But the tall, sardonic rider was for once in an easy mood. He drew a cigar from the pocket of his white shirt, thrust it between his teeth and bit off the end. He spat out the tip. Pony Deal struck a match and held it to the weed. Ringo took a deep draught, exhaled slowly.

"One thing you learn," he said thoughtfully, "is to never underestimate another man. I know Wyatt Earp for what he is—a good man with a six-gun. Guess he feels the same about me. Puts a sort of respect between us."

"He backed down that day in Tombstone," someone pointed out.

"Not because he was afraid," Ringo said. "He had a good reason. Just what it was, I don't know. Next time it could be different."

"You figure there'll be a next time?" Claiborne asked.

"Bound to be. Someday everything's going to shape up just right Then it will be Wyatt or me left standing."

"How about Doc Holliday?"

"Knew him in Kansas, too. He's another one you'd best walk careful around. He'll fight you anytime, anywhere you say. He's good, too, better than most because he's got something going for him. He doesn't give a damn whether he wins or loses in a gunfight. He's half dead with lung fever now so he figures a few days quicker won't matter."

Ringo paused, poured himself a drink. "And it doesn't—not for anybody. Man living with a gun in his hand all the time has to expect to die. He's a fool if he thinks he can go on forever. He might sail right along holding his own against the best of them. Then one day some little two-bit pipsqueak who hardly knows which end of a six-shooter the bullets come out of steps up and kills him.

"Makes a man figure he doesn't have a whole hell of a lot to say about it, so he might as well go right on ahead living the way he wants, doing what he likes and thinking and saying what he damn well pleases. He won't have much control over how he cashes in at the end regardless of what he tries to do."

"Sure thought I was done for back there at the O.K. Corral," Claiborne said. "And believe me, gents, I was doing all I could to keep breathing!"

Several men laughed. Ringo smiled. "You were up against the experts, Billy. How'd you manage to come out of it alive?"

"I took a couple of shots at Virgil Earp, then I saw quick I was in 'way over my head. About that time I got a glimpse of Sheriff Behan standing in the doorway of that picture gallery. He motioned for me to come that way—and I sure did, fast."

Ringo said, "Only two good gun hands in that scrap with the Earps and Holliday—the McLowrys. You didn't count. Neither did Ike and Billy Clanton."

"Guess that's right," Claiborne said. "The Earps were paying all their attention to Tom and Frank. Figured they'd better get them quick, I reckon."

"Just smart thinking, which is one thing you'd better do at a time like that if you want to stay alive," Ringo said. "The McLowrys were fast and better-than-average shots. They represented the big danger so they concentrated on them. Billy Clanton just happened to be close and in the way, so he caught a bullet, too."

There was silence after that. Somewhere in the back of the room a man swore, threw down his cards in protest to the ill luck that was running for him. The door opened and Phin Clanton, with Johnny Barnes, entered. They nodded, crossed to the bar, rubbing their hands together briskly to drive the cold from their fingers. Curly Bill stirred, brushed his hat to the back of his head, and sat up.

"You figure Earp and his crowd will get any tougher, once the weather clears up?" someone asked. "Hear talk of it in town."

Ringo said, "Can't see as it will make much difference, long as we hang together like we've been doing. Earp never gets the chance to pin anything on anybody."

"More to it now than talk," Phin Clanton said, picking up the conversation. "We just came up from Tombstone. They've had the governor down there, and that U.S. marshal, Dake, both. They've handed the whole ball of yarn over to Wyatt."

Curly Bill glanced sharply at Clanton. "Meaning what by that?"

"They've made Earp top lawman, even over John Behan. And they've appointed a bunch of deputies—federal deputies they call them. And they've raised fifteen thousand dollars for expenses."

"Told Wyatt they expected him to clean up the county," Johnny Barnes added.

"Could be a fair-sized chore," Brocius drawled.

"Old Judge Stillwell handed him a bunch of warrants and said he was to serve them best way he could. Made it plain he didn't care whether there was any prisoners brought in or not."

"One way of serving warrants." Curly Bill grinned. "Sounds like they're getting their dander up."

"They sure are, for a fact. Earp figures he's got the power now to do what he pleases. Only he's got a surprise coming."

"Surprise? What kind?"

"Ike's going to Behan and swear out murder charges again for the killing of Billy and the McLowrys. He figures that'll stop the Earps."

"He still trying to make that stick?" Brocius said. He swung his attention to Ringo. "What about it, Johnny? You think it'll work?"

Ringo wagged his head. "Never has before, why should

it now? Doubt if it even slows down Earp. You want to remember the Earp bunch was cleared by a grand jury and a judge once on those charges. Can't see any court listening to it again."

"Behan ain't going before any judge in Tombstone," Phin Clanton said. "He's taking it to a justice of the peace in Charleston, or maybe Contention."

Ringo tossed his cigar into a cuspidor. "Well, maybe they can make something out of it that way but my guess is that it's a waste of time. Anything that's going to be done about the Earps will have to be done by us—with six-guns."

"Him and his federal deputies are already out working," Clanton said then. "Caught some of the boys but really ain't got much on them. They'll get turned loose in a day or two. Run into Tom Coleman on our way up here. He was headin' for Mexico."

Brocius' big laugh boomed through the room. "Expect there'll be quite a few lining out for the border now. You see anything of Stilwell and Spence?"

"Nope. They supposed to be in town?"

"Around there somewhere. Frank had a little job him and Pete and some of the boys were going to pull."

"They sure better steer clear of the Earps. Stilwell's one of the bunch they'd sure like to nab, along with you and Ringo and a couple others."

"Earp's always give Galeyville a wide berth," Brocius said thoughtfully. "But with all that extra help he could change his thinking. Might be smart if we was to scatter, lay low until this thing blows over. What do you say, Johnny?"

"Good idea," Ringo agreed. "Ought to be safe down at your place on the Animas. And we could use Old Man Clanton's ranch. Right handy to the border."

"Fine," Brocius said. "Might as well move out now. All you boys that wants to come along, get your horses and gear. We'll pull out together. Couple of you circulate around, pass along the word."

Russian Bill got to his feet. "Count me out, Curly. I'm heading north. Still think I'd like to look around Lordsburg and some of those towns."

"Suit yourself. How about you, Johnny? You coming?"

Ringo shifted lazily in his chair. "Not much of a day for riding. Think I'll stay put until it clears up some."

"Me, too," Billy Claiborne said quickly. "I don't see no call to go off and hide."

Curly Bill gave the boy a wide grin. "Right time for everything, sonny. I figure this is the right time to just drop out of sight."

The door slammed back, bounced against the wall, rattled noisily. Frank Patterson, one of the older members of the gang, who had been with Clanton from the beginning, strode into the room. His sudden entrance brought half a dozen men to their feet, all reaching for their guns. They relaxed gently when they recognized him.

"What the devil's wrong with you?" Curly Bill demanded, half angry.

"Hell's poppin' in town!" Patterson said. "Somebody tipped off Earp about Stilwell and Spence. He nabbed them cold, got them indicted. Now they're back, swearin' they're goin' to wipe out the whole Earp bunch. They want all you to ride in and give them a hand."

17

Curly Bill let out a long sigh. "So that's where they been. Who tipped off Wyatt?"

Patterson said, "Don't know. They've corraled quite a few of the boys. Was one of them, I reckon. And Joe Hill's turned hisself in. Shot off his mouth about everythin' he knows."

Brocius grunted. "Don't think he can tell Earp much. Thing that always stops the marshal is that he's never got any real proof to go on."

"Don't seem to make much difference now. They're after the boys whether they got proof or not."

Curly Bill considered that in silence. Then, "Who else is with Frank and Pete?"

"The breed and Hank Swilling. Frank said when you come, come after dark. They'll be waitin' for you at Pete's house in town."

Brocius nodded his understanding. "Ringo, Pony, and me can handle this," he said, turning to the others in the room. "Don't think it would be a smart idea for a whole bunch of us to go trampin' in. Bound to get spotted. Rest of you head on down to the Animas. Soon as this is over with we'll meet you there."

Ringo was on his feet, moving for the door. Brocius and Pony Deal followed. The others began to stir, now that the plan was set.

"We'll have to burn a little leather," Deal said as they crossed the landing. "Not too much time."

They mounted up and struck out along the well-beaten

trail that led through the Chiricahuas into Sulphur Springs Valley, and finally to Tombstone. They arrived well after dark and pulled up quietly at the Spence house. Stilwell, Indian Charlie, Swilling, and Spence awaited them.

"You sure you know what you're up to?" Curly Bill asked when they had gathered in the shadows of the low-roofed structure and Stilwell had outlined his plan.

"I'm sure," Stilwell said. "Nobody slaps me around the way Wyatt did and gets away with it. Besides, I got that other thing hanging over my head at Tucson. I ain't got a prayer if I have to go back there and Wyatt testifies against me."

"Might be smarter just to drop out of sight for a spell."

"Not me. I'm out to settle with the Earps—the whole push."

Curly Bill glanced at Ringo. "How do you feel about it, Johnny?"

"I'd say let's go ahead," the tall outlaw answered. "Earp's asking for it. Let's give it to him."

"If we don't stop him we can all just saddle up and forget this country," Swilling said.

"All right. What's the next move?"

Stilwell said, "Morgan and Wyatt are at a show in Schieffelin Hall. Virgil's still laid up in bed at the hotel. The other two are around somewhere, but they don't count. It's Wyatt and Morgan we want right now—and sure got to get."

"That," John Ringo said softly, "is the important thing. You better be sure this first try works. If it fails, or turns out a halfway job, there'll be hell to pay."

"It'll work, far as Morgan and Wyatt are concerned,"

Pete Spence said.

"What do we do?" Curly Bill asked.

"You and Ringo and Pony scatter out along Fremont. One of you look after the horses. Rest of us will keep an eye on Schieffelin Hall. When the Earps come out, we'll pick 'em off."

"Be a crowd," Brocius said. "Could be easy to miss."

"We'll spot them," Stilwell said, "but just in case we don't, or we run into trouble, you and Johnny and Pony will be waiting there on Fremont. We'll sucker them into following us that way. Be easy for you to cut down on them."

"Ought to work all right," Curly Bill said.

"Then we're all set," Stilwell announced. "Let's get over—"

He stopped as a figure loomed up in the shadows. A voice said, "Frank, the Earps ain't over at the Hall no more. They left. Morgan's at Hatch's pool parlor and Wyatt went on to the hotel."

"Damn!" Stilwell muttered feelingly. "How'd it happen they left so early?"

"Show's over, that's why. You can still get to Morg, easy. Just go around to that alley behind Hatch's. You can see him through the glass in the door."

"Wyatt's there now with Morgan," another voice spoke up from the darkness. "Just saw him leave the hotel and head over there."

"Who're these men?" Curly Bill asked suddenly, his tone slightly alarmed and disturbed.

Stilwell said, "Couple of boys who've been keeping tabs on the Earps for me. Don't worry. They can be trusted."

"Then why don't they step out so's we can see who they are? Never liked dealing with a man who wouldn't show his face."

"Better nobody knows them," Stilwell said.

"Maybe so," Brocius muttered, dissatisfied. "Point that bothers me is they know who we are."

"I'll stand good," Stilwell said. Then, "Reckon this calls for a little change—even makes it easier, I'd say. Pete, you and Hank come with me. We'll go around to that alley. You, too, Charlie. Curly, how about you and Pony watching the front of Hatch's place, just in case we miss and they come busting out that way. Johnny, you stay put with the horses. All right?"

"Your show," Brocius said, "but let's get on with it."

They moved off into the night, Ringo leading the horses into the deep shadows where they would not be noticed yet were quickly available. He turned then, watched Pony Deal and Brocius merge into the darkness along Allen Street. It was late and the sounds of the town had died down, except for shouting and clapping coming from the Bird Cage Theatre, and a piano in one of the saloons. He eased a little farther toward the intersection, to where he had a better view of the street. Stilwell and the others had continued on to the rear of the billiard hall.

Minutes dragged by. Two riders entered the town, rode down the center of Allen Street, turned right at Third, heading for Dunbar's Corral. Somewhere a child was crying, and a dog barked steadily, insistently. Curly Bill materialized out of the night. He halted beside Ringo.

"Don't like this. Taking too long. Think I'll go have a look." He moved off again.

Alone once more, Ringo rode out the moments. And then suddenly the night erupted with the blast of gunfire. It was followed by a brief silence, shattered quickly by three more shots that echoed across the hush. Ringo wheeled to the horses, freed the leathers. He separated them in his hands and waited. He heard the hard pound of boot heels, of men running toward him. Stilwell appeared first. Next came Brocius, closely followed by the others. Pony Deal trotted in from the street.

"We got Morgan," Stilwell said, going to the saddle in a single bound. "Not sure about Wyatt."

"Missed him," Curly Bill said, his voice heavy with disgust. "That was him shooting through the door at us."

"Well, I sure ain't hanging around to find out," Stilwell said. "Best thing we can all do is get to Tucson fast, have us an alibi all cooked up and ready."

Ringo made no move to mount. "You're not certain about Wyatt?"

"No. Saw one bullet hit the wall right above his head. Don't know if any of the others got him or not. We were all throwing lead right smart there for a bit."

Allen Street had come alive. Men were rushing about, shouting, yelling questions. Lights were flaring up in shop windows. Someone was bellowing for Sheriff Behan.

"You all pull out," Ringo said. "I'll hang around a few minutes longer, see what I can learn."

"Suit yourself," Brocius said. "If Wyatt ain't dead, he'll be raking this town with a fine-tooth comb in another ten minutes. And if he is, they'll likely be doing it anyway. Could be sticking your neck out mighty far."

"Nobody will see me," Ringo said. "*Adios.* See you on

the Animas."

The others pulled about and moved off into the night, walking their horses at the start so no hoofbeats would sound and give them away. Ringo waited until they were gone and then, keeping to the shadows, walked to where he could see Hatch's poolroom. Several men had gathered in the front and he pushed in nearer to where he could hear what was being said.

"Morg's dyin'," a voice remarked. "Bullet went clean through him."

"Somebody said it killed a man standing behind him."

"Yeah. Name of George Berry."

"They sent for Virgil and the other two brothers. Guess Doc Goodfellow figures there ain't time to even move him."

"How about Wyatt?"

"Fit to be tied, and takin' it mighty hard. Reckon some of them bullets was meant for him, only he just happened to lean over and they missed. Three, maybe four men hidin' in the alley, they figure."

"Anybody see for sure who they were?"

"No, but Wyatt says he knows. Said he was going to get the ones who done it."

"Here comes Virgil now. . . ."

Ringo swung his attention toward the Cosmopolitan Hotel. Virgil Earp, supported at either shoulder by brothers Jim and Warren, was coming slowly and painfully down the street. The crowd gathered in front of Hatch's parted to let them enter.

Ringo dropped silently back to where his horse was tied. Stilwell and Curly Bill both had been right. They had been successful in their attempt to kill Morgan, but had failed where Wyatt was concerned. All hell would come loose at the seams now. Had both lawmen died there would be little, if anything, to worry about. A big hullabaloo would have followed, and then gradually tapered off, together with the campaign to clean up Cochise County. Now Wyatt, with revenge driving him mercilessly, would redouble his efforts to get the job done.

Ringo mounted his horse and walked him softly to the edge of town. Already the search was beginning. He could hear Wyatt Earp calling for volunteers, for his deputies, directing them to start beating through the streets and checking the houses and buildings.

Ringo reached the long canyon north of the settlement, where lay the cemetery. In the cold light the grave markers looked pale and ghostly. He halted, listened idly to the vague, remote sounds of activity in Tombstone.

His horse was too beat for the trip to the Animas. Or even back to Galeyville. He needed to go somewhere near and rest, at least until daylight. Curly Bill and Pony Deal would be facing the same problem. They certainly would not be riding on to Tucson with Stilwell and the others. But a man would be a fool to hang around Tombstone with matters the way they presently were. Wyatt and his deputies, in the frame of mind they undoubtedly were in, would check every square foot of ground in and adjacent to Tombstone.

Charleston—that was the answer. Swing wide of the town, get down along the San Pedro River, and ride south to Charleston. Put up for the night at Jerry Barton's, or maybe Ayers' place. Then, in the morning, head east.

He touched the horse with his spurs, sent him moving off into the star-shot night.

18

That next morning, as John Ringo rode leisurely eastward from Charleston, Wyatt Earp acted swiftly. He sought out Fred Dodge, one of the principal members of the law-and-order group.

"I'm calling a posse together and going after Morg's killers," he said. "I know who they are and I've got arrest warrants for every one of them in my pocket. I'm just hoping they'll be fools enough to resist."

He spent that Sabbath morning getting matters organized, the afternoon escorting Morgan's body, accompanied by Jim Earp, to the railhead, from which it was to be shipped to California for burial.

When that was accomplished he returned to Tombstone and finished laying his plans. The first thing on the list was to arrange for the crippled Virgil. All the bars were down now; it was a fight to the bitter end with the outlaws, and to leave Virgil, practically helpless and alone, would be an open invitation for the killers to walk in and account for another Earp.

He talked it over with his brother. "I'll be gone a week, maybe more. I don't want to worry about you while I'm away. Best thing is for you to go on to California where the folks are. You'll be safe there."

"Whatever you think, Wyatt."

"I'll have to be at that coroner's inquest tomorrow morning. When that's over with I'll put you on the train."

Earp then began to make inquiries that, he hoped, would result in more definite information on the killers. He knew Frank Stilwell and Pete Spence were the chief instigators of the crime. There were others, but their actual identity was still unknown to him. Late that day he received word from J. B. Ayers, who operated a saloon in Charleston and worked as an undercover agent for Wells Fargo.

Sunday morning, early, Ayers reported, Stilwell, Spence, Hank Swilling, Curly Bill Brocius, and the half-breed, Indian Charlie, had ridden into town. They obtained fresh horses from Stilwell's livery stable. Then Stilwell, Spence and Swilling had struck off in the direction of Tucson. Brocius and the half-breed lined out for the Dragoons.

It was as Earp had figured. Stilwell, Spence, Curly Bill, Hank Swilling—and Indian Charlie. But that was only five. One witness claimed to have seen seven dark figures running off into the night. Another was sure there were nine. . . . No matter. All were guilty in his eyes—every last man who ran with the Cowboy gang. And all would pay equally for their crimes.

Monday morning brought a telegram from the Tucson authorities, to whom he had made inquiry earlier. Frank Stilwell, Spence, and Swilling—and Ike Clanton—were in that city. The first three had arrived ahead of Clanton. Earp gave the presence of Ike with the others brief thought. It was possible Clanton was involved; he could be one of the missing number.

He attended the inquest, where the jury decided without much deliberation that Morgan Earp's death "was caused . . . from a gunshot or pistol wound on the night of March 18, 1882, by Pete Spence, Frank Stilwell, one John Doe Freeze, and an Indian called Charlie, and another Indian, name unknown."

They had been aided in arriving at their verdict and in specifying names by Pete Spence's wife, who came forward at the inquest and told the panel of the visitors who had called on her husband the night of the murder. Some she had recognized. "John Doe Freeze" was a mystery but it was assumed he was the person who kept Stilwell and the others informed as to the movements of the Earps.

Wyatt went into action immediately. The best strategy, as always, was to move first and fast. He called together his official federal deputies, who now included his brother Warren; Doc Holliday; Jack Johnson, usually known as "Turkey Creek"; Sherman McMasters; and Texas Jack Vermillion. They loaded up Virgil and his wife and escorted them to Contention. There, Wyatt, accompanied by Holliday, also boarded the train, after directing the posse to remain where they were until he returned.

In continuing on to Tucson, via rail, Earp had a dual purpose in mind. Stilwell and the others were reportedly in that city. They would not be expecting him to come by that route, would believe instead that he would arrive on horseback with a full posse at his command—if he came at all. Thus there was a good chance to close in on them unnoticed.

And there was the matter of Virgil. Since the train would halt in Tucson for dinner, the killers, possibly knowing that Virgil was aboard, would make their try at murdering another Earp. Therefore he needed protection until the cars pulled out for California.

The latter proved to be the case. Wyatt, searching the

railroad yards, came upon Frank Stilwell and three more shadowy figures waiting in ambush. They scattered at Earp's unexpected appearance but Wyatt managed to run one down, kill him with a blast from the Wells Fargo shotgun he was carrying. It was Stilwell. Virgil's train moved off and Doc Holliday and Wyatt combed the area for the three other men but failed to turn them up. They then checked with Tucson's deputy marshal about the information wired earlier to Earp.

"I saw Stilwell, Spence, and Swilling. They got in yesterday morning. Ike Clanton came later. Ike's received several telegrams from your town. He knew you were on that train. Somebody kept him posted."

Earp and Holliday again made a search through the city, found none of the men they sought. They caught the next train back to Benson and rejoined the posse, waiting as ordered at Contention. From there they rode to Tombstone, where the news of Stilwell's death had preceded them. In need of sleep, Earp went to his room at the Cosmopolitan. Late in the afternoon, the telegraph operator, a close friend, awakened him.

"Thought you ought to know about this wire before I deliver it, Wyatt. It's for Behan, from Tucson. It says you and Doc Holliday are being accused of murdering Frank Stilwell."

"What?" Earp shouted, coming to his feet. "Who sent it?"

"Signed by Ike Clanton. He swore out the warrant."

Earp dressed hurriedly and hunted up his attorney, Colonel Herring. He told him of the telegram Behan was about to receive—the delivery of which was being delayed by the operator at Wyatt's request for another hour.

"Want you to wire Bob Paul in Tucson," Earp said. "Tell him I'll surrender to him any time he says—but never to anybody else."

Herring agreed and sent word to the lawman. Earp passed along instructions for the federal deputies to assemble and be ready to ride on short notice. He returned to his room, where he put his affairs in order, and then, late, he was advised that Sheriff Behan was below in the lobby and wished to see him.

He strapped on his guns and went down the stairs. Dave Neagle, the town marshal, was with the lawman. In front of the hotel, in Allen Street, half a dozen more of Behan's deputies, all armed, waited. Earp grinned as he noted the federal posse, captained by Doc Holliday, also standing by.

Neagle offered his services but Earp waved him aside. "If Behan wants to arrest me, let him try."

The sheriff considered for a moment, then turned and went into the street, where his deputies had lined up. Earp, followed by the posse members, walked out of the lobby and headed for his horse.

"Wyatt!" Behan called. "I want to see you!"

Earp wheeled about. "If you aren't careful," he said, "you're going to see me once too often."

He strode on, reached the horses. He swung onto the saddle, the posse following. The sheriff and his deputies remained standing in the street. The Earp party rode off, and two miles out of town, Earp brought it to a halt.

"Too late now to ride far," he said. "We'll bed down here for the night."

When camp had been made and the men were sitting

back, relaxed and smoking their pipes and cigars, Doc Holliday settled down beside Earp.

"Wyatt, you think Sheriff Paul will show up from Tucson to arrest us on that murder charge?"

Earp shook his head. "Doubt it. Paul knows the situation here, and he'll take me at my word. He knew Frank Stilwell worked for Behan and he'll realize the whole thing was cooked up to delay us, to keep us from laying any more of the Cowboy gang by the heels."

"You think he figures it was murder?"

"He knows it wasn't. But he's the sheriff there and he has to act when a warrant is sworn out. Expect he laughed in Ike's face when he showed up."

"Too bad we didn't have more on Ike. Would have been a good chance for Paul to grab him."

"Rider coming," someone warned.

It was a messenger from Tombstone. He brought Earp a copy of the coroner's jury findings. It was much the same as before except that now Hank Swilling was named as one of the men involved in Morgan Earp's killing. It also said the half breed's true identity was Florentino Cruz.

The next morning, March 22, 1882, as they were preparing to move out, a second messenger arrived.

"John Behan's making up a posse to follow and arrest you and Holliday," the man said. "He's getting all the Cowboy bunch he can find to ride in it. Ike and Phin Clanton are among them."

Earp thought for a minute. Then, "Well, we'll make it easy for him. Tell him I'll be at the old powder house at dark. If he wants to try and make an arrest, I'll be there waiting."

"Something else you ought to know."
"About Morgan's murder?"
"Yes. Johnny Ringo was mixed up in it, too."

19

Ringo. . . .
Earp stared at the paper in his hand. "Didn't think he'd be in on that kind of a deal. Not his way, usually."
"You've got to remember this was Stilwell's idea," Holliday said. "Probably he was calling the shots. His and maybe Curly Bill's."
"How about Curly Bill Brocius?"
The messenger said, "He was there, too. And he was back in Tombstone last night. Rode out after talking to Behan. We'll try to keep you informed on things like that, marshal."
Ringo and Curly Bill. The list was becoming more complete. If they were there, likely Pony Deal had been close by, also. The messenger departed but before they could get under way, additional word came.
"That half-breed, Indian Charlie—Cruz his name is—you'll find at Pete Spence's ranch. A cowpuncher just rode in. Said he saw him and some others up there."
Earp's face darkened. "That's where we go first. I want him."
The posse mounted and hurried to Spence's place. They found several more known members of the Cowboys gathered at a water hole nearby. They closed in. The half-breed attempted to escape into the rocks but a well-placed rifle shot by Sherman McMasters seared his leg and he

promptly surrendered.

"Are you Florentino Cruz?" Earp asked when the man was dragged before him.

The Indian pretended he could not speak English. McMasters, fluent in Spanish, took over as interpreter.

Indian Charlie, under relentless questioning, readily admitted his part in the murder of Morgan Earp. He named Ringo, Curly Bill, Ike Clanton, Stilwell, Pete Spence, and Swilling as the men who had pulled it off. Ringo had stood watch at the horses, he said. The "John Doe Freeze" mentioned in the coroner's report was a bartender who had worked with Stilwell. He did not know his name.

The half-breed also told of other matters. In the attempt to kidnap and kill Mayor Clum, the leaders had been Ringo, the two Clantons, Curly Bill, Swilling, and Bill Claiborne. And when Virgil Earp was shot, it was again John Ringo, Stilwell, Hank Swilling, Ike Clanton, and a man he did not know who had made the effort.

Earp swore softly. He had felt all along that Ringo was more involved in the various incidents than it had appeared. But there was never any definite information linking him to the affairs. He should have just assumed it, however; he should have remembered that Ringo and Curly Bill were never long separated. He turned to McMasters.

"Ask him why he wanted to kill my brothers and me. We never harmed him—not any time I recall."

Cruz' reply was, "Those men were all my friends. They said we would make lots of money if you were dead. They gave me twenty-five dollars to help."

All compassion left Wyatt Earp at the moment of that

statement. To McMasters he said, "Hand him his gun. Tell him I'm giving him a chance for his life. I'll count to three and draw. He can go for his pistol any time he pleases."

Earp put three bullets into Indian Charlie before the half-breed could get off his first shot. Wyatt then sent a rider on to Tombstone to notify the coroner of the Indian's death, and led the posse on to the old powder house near the settlement, where he had promised he would be at nightfall.

Several members of the Safety Committee were there waiting. Behan was moving fast, they said. He had appointed Curly Bill a deputy and the man had formed a posse which included Pony Deal, Frank Patterson, and half a dozen more members of the Cowboy clan. Last reports placed them somewhere on the Babocomari, a rough and overgrown section of the Whetstone Mountains. Behan himself had organized a second group—chief among whom was John Ringo.

Ringo again. Earp shook his head. "What about Bob Paul?"

"He notified us that Behan was acting without authority from him. Said that when he wanted you, he'd let you know."

Earp nodded in satisfaction. "Figured that's the way Paul would look at it. Any idea where Behan was going when he took out his posse?"

"No. Only information we've got is that Curly Bill and his bunch are on the Babocomari, somewhere close to the east water hole."

"Then I reckon that's the logical place for us to look for him," Earp said.

They pulled out early that next morning, cutting straight

across the San Pedro Valley to the blue-shadowed Whetstones in the west. Their exact destination in that area was Iron Springs, and it was a hot, dusty thirty-five-mile ride. They would camp there, Earp had told the Safety Committee, and ordered certain supplies and an amount of cash money for expenses to be sent there to him.

It was also the heart of the country where Brocius was said to be, and as they drew nearer, after leaving Warren Earp at a fork in the road to await the messenger from Tombstone, he called upon the deputies to proceed with caution. So far he had seen no evidence of other horsemen, but Earp was wary. If Curly Bill and his followers were around, they most likely would be at the water hole.

Drawing near, Earp dismounted. He approached on foot, shotgun ready in his hands. When he reached the point where he could look down onto the basin with its spring, two men leaped to their feet and faced him. One was Curly Bill. The other Pony Deal.

The two deputies who had been directly behind Earp wheeled out of the line of fire. Brocius, also carrying a shotgun, fired hastily. The double-barreled charge whipped at Earp's coattails. The lawman lunged to one side, fired an answering blast. It caught the big, curly-haired man in the chest, almost cut him into two parts. Beyond him Earp could see Pony Deal and about six more of the outlaws racing to gain the shelter of the trees and rocks. He opened up on them with his revolver.

For a time there was only confusion while the opposing forces exchanged gunshots and endeavored to get reorganized. Pony Deal seemed to have taken over command of the Cowboys and Wyatt could hear him directing them to positions of advantage.

He discovered then that one of his own members, Texas Jack Vermillion, had lost his horse in the initial flurry of bullets. Earp continued to throw lead at the trees where the outlaws were hiding while Vermillion stripped the gear from his dead animal. After Doc Holliday had come from the rocks behind which the remainder of the deputies had taken shelter and carried Texas Jack to safety, Wyatt retreated.

He was unhurt although half a dozen bullets had ripped through his clothing, nicked his saddle and shotgun. His horse had a slight wound but nothing so serious as to disable him. Holliday wanted to rush Deal and his men. Several others backed the proposal. With Curly Bill dead the outlaws would be rattled, ready to run. It would be smart to press the advantage.

Earp turned down the suggestion. "They're spotted in the rocks and trees, and well hid out," he said. "We'd have to cross open ground to reach them and that would make us easy targets. Forget it. Besides, we've got to water our horses and get another for Texas Jack. Best thing we can do is drop back to where we left Warren."

The youngest Earp was still waiting at the split in the trail. The Tombstone courier had not yet put in an appearance with the needed supplies.

"What was all the shooting?" Warren asked.

Wyatt told him. "I got Curly Bill," he finished. "One more killer accounted for."

"It'll sure put a crimp in John Behan," someone said.

"Stilwell, Indian Charlie, and now Curly Bill. I'd say we've made a good start at breaking up that outlaw gang."

Wyatt Earp was quiet for a long minute. "A good start—that's about all," he said finally. "Remember, we've still got John Ringo and Pony Deal, the Clantons, Swilling, and plenty more."

"We'll find them, too."

"Finding them," Earp said quietly, "isn't all there is to it."

Turning back from Iron Springs, he led his posse of deputies away from the Whetstones to a new camp a few miles outside Tombstone. There he bivouacked and wrote a complete report of Curly Bill's death. He made two copies, sent one to the Safety Committee, the other to John Clum and the *Epitaph.* He also asked about the money and supplies he had requested.

A messenger returned shortly after, bringing the needed items. "Couldn't get through yesterday," he said. "Behan had a couple of men watching me. If I had left town, they'da known exactly where you were camping."

Earp nodded his understanding. "Any more news?"

"Ringo and Hank Swilling were seen up in the San Simon country this morning."

"The San Simon country?" Earp echoed. "How the devil could they have gotten clear up there?"

"Don't know, but the man who brought in the word said he was sure it was them."

Earp had his first doubts then as to the confession made by Indian Charlie. Thinking back on it he realized it would have been a physical impossibility for Ringo to have been all the places and taken part in the incidents the half-breed had credited to him. Perhaps Indian Charlie had disliked Ringo, which would not have been anything unusual. The tall outlaw seldom bothered to make friends.

"Ranchers are cooperating real good with us," the messenger said. "They keep sending in information fast as they come across something. They're mighty anxious to see this gang of outlaws and rustlers busted up. They're sure going to be happy when they hear about Curly Bill."

There was no doubt in anyone's mind that it was a major victory for the law-and-order faction. But Wyatt Earp was thinking of something else—what would John Ringo do when he learned his best and probably only real friend was dead?

20

It was not John Ringo the rancher had noted in the San Simon Valley. He was with Sheriff John Behan's posse and continued to ride with it while the lawman probed, with no success, through the hills for Wyatt Earp and his party. Finally, low on supplies and saddle-weary, they returned to Tombstone.

One of the deputies met them as they pulled into Dexter's stables. "You hear the news? Earp killed Curly Bill!"

Ringo, in the act of coming off his worn horse, settled gently on his heels. His shoulders came back stiffly, his face tipped down as his eyes narrowed.

He murmured, "Earp—damn him—"

As the shock of the announcement began to stir the anger within him, he heard Behan speak.

"You sure about that?"

"Was in the paper—the *Epitaph.* And the Committee

got a report."

"I don't believe it," Behan said. "Who saw the body?"

"Nobody. When the coroner and some others went out to view it, it was gone."

"Just what I figured!" Behan exclaimed. "When they killed poor Indian Charlie, the body was there, wasn't it? Then why didn't they find Curly Bill? All some sort of a damn trick." The lawman pivoted to Ringo. "Don't know what's behind this, but I can guess. Wyatt's trying to split you boys up, start you running—"

Ringo was only partly listening. He thrust his foot into the stirrup, prepared to mount. Behan rushed forward in alarm.

"Where you going?"

"To find out for sure about Curly. If he's dead, I'm taking out after Wyatt—alone."

"Wait here," the lawman said quickly. "Best you let me handle this."

Ringo hesitated for a moment, then settled back. "All right," he said. "I'll wait thirty minutes."

He watched Behan move hurriedly off down the street. He should have forced Earp's hand, had it out with him before it got down to this, he realized. Earp had just been biding his time, awaiting a good opportunity for a showdown with Curly Bill—and him. It had probably been in the lawman's mind ever since he had arrived in Tombstone. Well, he'd get it now. If Curly were dead, Wyatt Earp would be brought to account—and he would go it alone. His chances for finding the marshal would be much better if he went by himself.

He saw Behan then, returning at a fast walk. The sheriff

was smiling as he came up.

"Just what I thought—no proof of it! Nobody knows if Curly Bill's dead. All they got is a note from Earp saying he did it, and that I don't believe. Neither does a lot of people."

Ringo felt some of the hard anger fade from his mind. He said, "Can't see why Earp would say it unless it was so."

"Not hard to understand," the sheriff replied, waving his hands. "With Curly Bill dead, it'll look like Wyatt's doing a big job. And, like I already said, a lot of the boys will cut and run, maybe even turn themselves in. Wyatt's a schemer but he's not fooling me."

Ringo considered the lawman thoughtfully. Behan could be right; it would be like Earp to come up with such a plan—and it was hard to believe the lawman was good enough to gun down Brocius, unless, of course, he caught him at a disadvantage.

"We'll rest up a bit and get fresh horses," Behan was saying. "Then we'll go after Earp again. Hank," he added, turning to Swilling, "I want you to go to Tucson. See Sheriff Paul. You saw Wyatt shoot Frank Stilwell. Add your name to that warrant calling for Earp's arrest. We'll force Paul to act. Rest of you go on home, or over to a hotel, and take it easy. I'll call you when were ready to ride."

The posse broke up and the members moved off to do the sheriff's bidding. Ringo remained. Behan glanced at him, frowned.

"That suit you, Johnny?"

Ringo, leaning against the wall of the livery stable, nodded. "It's all right, but if Curly's dead—"

"He's not," the sheriff stated confidently. "You can be damn sure of that."

Swilling did as he was ordered. Immediately word of it was wired to Tombstone, thus pinpointing his whereabouts for Earp and his deputies. Swilling would be returning by rail, the marshal was advised. It would be a simple matter to intercept him when the train reached Benson.

That next day, March 22, 1882, as Earp was breaking camp, Behan and his twenty-man posse were also getting under way. When they rode out they left the town in a turmoil over the question of Curly Bill's death. The sheriff had succeeded in clouding the matter completely. The *Nugget* had come out with an offer to pay a one-thousand-dollar reward to any man who could prove Brocius dead. The *Epitaph* countered with a two-thousand-dollar offer for anyone who could prove he was not.

In any event Behan had accomplished his purpose; the Cowboy faction still stood firmly together—and behind him. And John Ringo had not broken away to undertake a personal vengeance search on his own.

The strategy Behan had hoped might work on Sheriff Bob Paul, however, had gone amiss. Paul had arrived from Tucson but he refused to join Behan's posse. All members of that group, Paul declared, were hostile to Wyatt Earp and Doc Holliday, and a meeting with them could not result in lawful arrests but only in bloodshed. He then caught the train back to Tucson.

John Behan was not deterred. He began the quest with the men he had appointed deputies, heading off into the hill determinedly. They called at several ranches, inquired as to the possibility of the Earp party having been in the area. Information was hard to obtain.

Ringo, riding at the head of the posse with Behan and Ike Clanton, could see what was happening. The report of Curly Bill's death, despite the sheriff's denial, was having a strong effect upon the residents of Cochise County—outside the town limits of Tombstone. They believed Wyatt Earp, distrusted Behan. Previously, as long as the big, reckless, black-haired Brocius rode the countryside as chief of the outlaws, there had been fear. Now, with him dead, a new courage had been born.

And John Ringo was finding his own interest lagging. If Curly Bill were dead there seemed little point in pressing the so-called search. Better he pull out and alone, bide his time until he could meet Wyatt face to face and square things for Brocius. He had his doubts as to what John Behan would do should they overtake the marshal and his deputies, anyway. He wished they would encounter Pony Deal or some of the men who had been with Curly Bill. Then he could find out for certain what had happened, and settle in his own mind what he should do.

"We're wasting time," he said to Behan, late that morning. "We could ride these hills and flats for a month and never cross Earp's trail if he had in mind to dodge us. Fact is, we don't even know he's in this part of the county!"

"He is," the sheriff assured him. "Got a tip he planned to stop at Hooker's Sierra Bonita Ranch. That's where we're going now."

"Where'd you get that information?"

"From Swilling," Behan replied, ducking his head at the man. "He picked it up at Benson after he jumped the train when Earp started to search it."

Ringo shrugged. "Well, if we don't find him there, I'm pulling out. If Wyatt killed Curly, I'll look him up on my own. I've got my doubts that he did—Curly would never let himself get caught flatfooted the way that report says."

"Way I look at it, too," Behan said. "Curly Bill was no greenhorn, not by a long shot. Earp wouldn't get him that easy."

They reached the Sierra Bonita holdings early the next morning. Hooker, with several of his ranch hands, waited for them in the yard.

"Colonel," Behan said, as they pulled to a halt, "we're officers of the law on official business. We need food for ourselves and our mounts. I'm asking you to accommodate us."

Hooker nodded. "Get down. I'll see that something is fixed for you."

"We're obliged," Behan said. "Now, one more thing. I have warrants for the arrest of Wyatt Earp and Doc Holliday. Have you seen any signs of them and their party?"

Hooker bristled instantly. "If I had I wouldn't tell you!"

"I warn you," Behan said sternly, "you'd be protecting murderers against officers of the law."

Several of Hooker's men closed in beside the old rancher. He looked over Behan's deputies through half-shut eyes.

"Officers of the law!" he echoed scornfully. "Outside of you and Harry Woods there, I expect every one of them has at some time rustled my beef and stolen my horses. Its nothing but a posse of outlaws!"

"Only men in Tombstone with guts enough to go after

Earp and Holliday," Behan countered.

"Doesn't change a thing—they're still a pack of outlaws and thieves!"

Suddenly Ike Clanton drew his pistol. "Damn him! He knows where Earp's hiding! Let's make him tell!"

One of Hooker's riders spoke up, his voice low and promising. He had his gun out and leveled at Clanton's belly.

"Put that pistol away! You can't come onto a man's place and talk to him like that. And if you keep on, you'll get a fight right here before you ever find Wyatt Earp!"

Ike slid his weapon back into its holster and turned aside. The men of the posse and Hooker's riders relaxed. The cook shouted something from the back of the house.

"Grub's ready," Hooker said gruffly, and stamped off.

Behan and his men trailed after him, took places at a table prepared apart from the Sierra Bonita employees. When all had finished, the sheriff crossed to Hooker.

"Since you won't give me your help, I'm riding across the valley to Fort Grant and hire some Indian trackers. My deputies will wait here, if you don't mind."

"Do what you damn please," Hooker muttered.

Behan returned several hours later. He had been unsuccessful in obtaining assistance from the Fort's commander.

"All right," Hooker said, changing his mind. "I'll tell you where they are. Up on top of Reilly Hill, about three miles away. They're waiting for you—eight to your twenty-one. Go after them, sheriff! Wyatt said to tell you he'd be expecting you."

The interest of Ringo and Hank Swilling and several others perked up. Behan considered in thoughtful silence.

"Expect they're pretty well armed," he said, "and forted up on top of that hill. Be mighty hard to take."

"You've got plenty of guns," Hooker said. "And about three times as many men. Go on!"

Behan shook his head. "Just be a lot of useless killing. There's been too much of that already."

He ordered the posse to the saddle, pulled off a short distance and halted. He faced his men.

"We'd be fools to ride into a hornet's nest like Earp's got waiting for us. Best thing we can do is fall back to Tombstone, try and draw him out."

Ringo swore in disgust. Ike Clanton objected loudly but the others said nothing. Earp and his federal Deputies occupied a most formidable position. It would be folly to ride up the slopes of Reilly Hill under the muzzles of the lawmen's guns. They swung about and returned to Tombstone. Earp, however, failed to take the bait; he did not follow.

Pete Spence was in Behan's office when the posse walked in. "I'm giving myself up," he said. "Tired of dodging Earp and all them deputies."

Behan studied the harried-looking man for a moment, then shrugged. "All right, get in one of the cells. But you'll have to look after yourself. I'm going to be busy."

Ringo, fed up with the whole thing, glanced at Hank Swilling. "Sounds like good advice—look out for yourself. I'm taking it, and heading for Galeyville. Maybe Curly will be there. If he's not, I'm riding on to the Animas."

"Count me in," Swilling said.

"And me," Clanton added.

21

The spring wind was cold as they rode across the broad Sulphur Springs Valley to the Chiricahuas.

"Thing we'd better do is lay low in Galeyville until we can collect the boys," Ike Clanton said. "Then we can move in again. I ain't through with Wyatt yet—not by a damn sight."

"What boys?" Hank Swilling asked dryly. "Earp's got them scattered from hell to hallelujah. What ain't in jail are on the run to Mexico or somewhere."

"You think so? I figure you're wrong. My guess is we'll find some of them already waiting for us at Galeyville. Others will come drifting in pretty fast. Don't you think so, Johnny?"

Ringo shifted on his saddle. He had done so much riding in the past week that his bones and muscles ached with a dull insistence.

"Hank's right. Wyatt's outguessed Behan, outplayed him right down the line. And if Curly Bill's dead, then the gang's finished."

"We don't need him!" Clanton flared. "I can run the outfit good as he."

Ringo laughed, a short, derisive sound. "Yeah, you can run it right straight into the graveyard."

They continued on in silence after that. A short time later they entered Galeyville and pulled to a halt at the hitch rack fronting the saloon where they ordinarily gathered. They dismounted stiffly, cold and hard-tempered, and went inside. The town was abnormally quiet and all three men, suddenly aware of that quality, moved with a wariness they customarily abandoned when in the settlement. They bellied up to the bar in the deserted saloon and Ringo called for a bottle and glasses.

"Anybody around?" he asked.

The bartender shook his head. "Not for three, four days. They all pulled out."

"Going where?"

The man shrugged. "Who knows? Mexico—Texas—New Mexico. Maybe even California. Nobody done much talking."

"Earp?"

"Yeah. He sure put the fear of God into them!"

Hank Swilling laughed. "Appears he scared off everybody else, too. Place looks locked up tighter'n a Shalamite town on Sunday morning."

"Oh, folks are around," the bartender said, polishing at the surface of the counter. "Only thing is nobody ain't sure about what's happening next." He paused, smiled weakly at Ringo. "Meaning not to be smart alec, but way it is now, folks don't know whether you boys will be running the town, or Earp and his law crowd. So everybody is being real careful what they say or do."

Ringo took a long swallow from his glass. He lowered it, stared moodily at the remaining liquid. If he had heard the bartender's explanation he gave no sign of it. He raised his eyes to the man.

"You hear anything about Curly Bill?"

"Only that he's dead. Earp got him with a shotgun, they say."

Swilling poured himself a healthy shot from the bottle.

"Behan claims that's a lie. Says Wyatt started the rumor to split the outfit up and start the boys running."

Again the bartender's shoulders twitched. "Well, I only know what I heard. And if that's what Earp wanted to do, he sure done it. You're the first of the old bunch I've laid eyes on since the word got out."

Ringo took the bottle and his glass, moved to a table. Swilling and Clanton followed. They sat down in silence and began to drink.

Swilling said, "How we going to find out for sure about Curly Bill?"

Ringo considered his drink. "Ride down and see if he's at his place on the Animas, for one thing. If he's not, then go on to the Babocomari. That's where he was headed."

"Country between here and there will be crawling with lawmen. Could run into trouble."

"Man is careful, he can slip by."

"Let him find us," Clanton grumbled. "Anyway, I still say we can run things without him. Long as Behan stays sheriff, we got nothing to worry—"

The door opened. Pony Deal, looking trail-worn and haggard, entered. He saw the three men at the table, grinned broadly, and started toward them.

"Damn glad to see you birds!" he said, settling down in the vacant chair. "Was beginning to think I was the last one of the bunch left in the country!"

Ringo's fingers reached out, fastened on Deal's wrist. "What's the straight dope on Curly Bill? You were with him."

"Dead," Pony said without hesitation. "Wyatt got him. Charge of buckshot right in the belly."

A low sigh slipped from Ringo's lips. "What we heard was true. Behan lied."

Pony Deal tipped the bottle to his mouth, took a long drink. Then, "Behan? Don't know what he had to do with it, but I was there. Curly and me were squatting down at the water hole when Earp and his posse sneaked in on us. We jumped and run for it. Curly took a shot at Wyatt and missed. Wyatt didn't."

"Anybody else get hit?" Clanton asked.

"Couple of the boys. Johnny Barnes was the worst. Took a bullet in the chest. Doubt if he makes it."

Ringo, seemingly still disbelieving that Brocius could be dead, said, "You're sure about Curly?"

"I'm sure, Johnny. Helped bury him myself on Frank Patterson's place."

"Guess that finishes it," Ringo said in a quiet voice. "And leaves me with a chore to do."

"You're right, far as everything being finished is concerned," Pony Deal declared. "Done a little listening around Tombstone last night. The new governor is talking about sending in the Army to help Earp. They've made up their minds to take over Cochise County and run it the way they want. The ranchers are even sending in men to ride with Wyatt."

"Where's he now?"

"Headed this way. Galeyville's about the only place he hasn't combed through." Deal paused, looked closely at Ringo. "Johnny, if you're thinking to square things for Curly, forget it. With the posse Wyatt's got, you'd not get within a half mile of him."

Ringo said, "Maybe."

"I'm telling you straight. Let it slide. There'll come another day."

"But what about Behan?" Clanton protested. "He's still running things, ain't he?"

"Behan's through. Nobody's paying any mind to him."

"You can forget him, too," Ringo said. "He was friendly to us for a reason—he needed our backing in his fight with Earp to control Tombstone and the county. Wyatt has the upper hand now. My guess is Behan will turn against us, make a big show of it, and try to save his own skin."

Pony Deal nodded. "Maybe, but he's still trying to stop Earp. Says he's going to serve those murder warrants somehow."

"Never do it," Swilling said. "Don't think he's got the guts to try it alone. Besides, Wyatt's too smart to let him."

There was silence after that as each man wrestled with his own thoughts. Outside the wind was rising steadily, shouldering against the flimsy building in sporadic gusts that shivered the doors and windows, filled the room with a desolate sound.

"Stilwell . . ." Ringo muttered after a time. "If he'd listened to Curly Bill and not forced Earp's hand, things might still be going right. We had a good setup here until he got big ideas."

"For sure," Swilling said morosely. "Point is, what's next? We move on like the rest of the boys?"

"No!" Ike Clanton shouted, smacking the table top with his knotted fist. "We don't! I'm not through with Earp—and he ain't running me out of the country!"

"Don't be a fool," Ringo said. "Pony's right. Man would be crazy to buck Wyatt now, backed up the way he is. Let him work out his string. It'll grow old mighty fast and he'll quit. Got a score of my own to settle with him now, but I'll bide my time."

"Sure," Swilling said. "Let him think he's driven us out of the territory. Then when it's all blown over, we can come back."

Clanton agreed reluctantly. "Expect I know this country good as he does, maybe better. Be no chore to hide out. But I'll trail along with the rest of you, if that's what you want. But I'm coming back—and I'm getting the bunch together again. No reason why we can't have things all our way around here, just like they were."

Ringo shook his head slowly. "You're fooling yourself, Ike. The old days are gone. Tombstone's done for, and so is everything else around here. If you're looking for easy pickings like we had, you'd better find yourself a new town."

"Something we can talk about later," Pony Deal said, glancing toward the deserted, wind-swept street. "We better be pulling out of here. That posse can't be far away."

"Where we go?" Swilling asked. "Texas?"

Ringo said, "South—to Mexico."

Pony Deal got to his feet. "Sounds good to me, but let's get riding. Want to be a long way from here an hour from now."

"Let's go," Clanton said. "But why Mexico?"

Ringo arose lazily. "You think of any other place where we can stay close to Wyatt—and he still can't touch us?"

22

Earp and his federal posse swept across the Sulphur Springs Valley, swarmed through the foothills, probed the canyons and other known hideouts of the Cowboys, and came finally to the Galeyville stronghold.

They split into grim, determined groups and began to search the buildings. Earp himself, with three men, entered the saloon where Curly Bill had more or less maintained headquarters. The lawman faced the bartender.

"We know Ringo and Ike Clanton are around here. Could be Swilling and Claiborne and some of the others, too. Where are they? Either I get an answer or I'll burn this place to the ground."

The bartender returned the marshal's stare. "They pulled out. Been gone quite a spell."

Earp glanced meaningfully about the saloon. "This place would go up mighty fast, once a match was set to it."

"Help yourself, Mr. Earp," the bartender said indifferently. "Still won't find any of them, and for one good reason—they flat ain't here!"

Earp wheeled abruptly and went through the doorway onto the board landing that fronted the building. Along the short street, whipped by the cold, disagreeable wind, he could see his deputies going from one structure to another, talking to the various persons they encountered. Apparently they were getting the same answer he had received from the bartender. Then, in ones and twos, they reported back to him. McMasters was the last.

"Nobody," the deputy said. "If Ringo was here, he's

gone now. What's next?"

Wyatt Earp looked toward the north. "We keep riding," he said. "We'll cover the San Simon, the San Luis; we'll go clear to Lordsburg, if need be. I want this finished—all the way."

They rode out and for almost a month they ranged back and forth, followed out leads, chased shadows until finally, late in April, Wyatt himself agreed they were spending themselves uselessly. Ringo, Clanton, Hank Swilling, Pony Deal, Claiborne, and all the others of note had evidently dropped from the face of the earth. Just where they had gone, aside from Mexico, was anybody's guess. One thing was certain; they were nowhere in southeastern Arizona.

Earp doubled back to Tombstone, sending word ahead for the Safety Committee to meet him at the usual rendezvous, the powder storage house. He had grown tired of the saddle and he wanted an end to trouble. More important, he wanted the murder charge still standing against him and Doc Holliday cleared up.

"Doc and I have decided to go on to Tucson and surrender to Sheriff Paul," he said when they were all together again at the appointed place. "Only way I can see to clean up those murder warrants."

"Be the wrong thing to do, Wyatt," one of the vigilante members, an attorney, said. "You've got to remember Behan has friends in Pima County—powerful friends. Chances are, even if you were cleared at a hearing on Frank Stilwell's death, they'd turn you over to Behan to face the warrants he's still carrying around."

"Behan hasn't given up yet," someone added. "Paul

would have to hand you and Doc over to him when he was through. And once Behan got you across the line into Cochise County, your lives wouldn't be worth a nickel."

"Then what's the answer?" Earp demanded impatiently. "I don't propose to spend the rest of my time with a murder charge hanging over my head!"

"I know how to settle it," Holliday murmured. "One little visit to Sheriff Behan—"

"The one thing neither of you should even think about doing," the attorney cut in hurriedly. "Be playing right into his hands. My advice is for you to go to another state, or territory—Colorado would probably be best—and give yourselves up to the authorities. Then we'll get busy here and persuade the new governor, Tritle, to file extradition papers on the strength of the Tucson warrants."

"How can that help?" Holliday asked. "We'll still have to show up in Tucson for a hearing."

"Only if the governor of Colorado, if that's where you go, honors the extradition request—which I doubt will happen. He'll look into the charge and once the facts are placed before him, he'll throw it all out as worthless. This puts the case at state-government level, rather than in the hands of the county officials. Behan won't have a thing to say about any part of it."

Earp said, "Sounds to me like the answer. You agree, Doc?"

Holliday nodded. "I'm ready to ride when you are."

"No time like now," Earp said.

Sherm McMasters spoke up. "We'll all just go along," he said. "The whole posse. Behan could get wind of this and make a try at heading you off before you reached the Colorado line. Besides, won't hurt to take one more good look for Ringo and his crowd before we call it quits."

They rode north that next morning. It was an uneventful journey and on May 10, 1882, Wyatt Earp telegraphed Sheriff Paul in Tucson that he was at Gunnison, Colorado, with Holliday, and both wished to surrender to him. Paul wired back instructions to continue on to Denver and there turn themselves over to the proper authorities. This was done and extradition processes were set in motion.

Governor Tritle, acting in accordance with suggestions from the Safety Committee, as well as law officials in Tucson, handed Sheriff Paul the necessary papers and dispatched him to Denver. Colorado's chief executive, F. W. Pitkin, held a hearing, listened to testimony, reviewed various affidavits and documents pertinent to the matter, and then, as predicted, refused to honor the extradition request. He could find no valid reason to hold for murder an officer of the federal government who had been acting merely in accord with his sworn duty.

That was the end of it for Wyatt Earp.

He elected not to return to Arizona, and the posse broke up when he announced his decision. A few went back to Tombstone, others remained in Colorado or headed on for Utah. Wyatt, his brother Warren, and Holliday drifted on to the Colorado mining town of Trinidad, where Bat Masterson was operating a saloon and gambling house. Holliday, restless, pushed farther into new fields, eventually to die peacefully in bed of tuberculosis at Glenwood Springs.

The two Earps moved on to Gunnison, then booming to spectacular heights. Wyatt was reported to have pyramided a three-hundred-dollar bank roll into ten thousand at the faro tables. From there he wandered westward, going from one town to another aimlessly.

He never returned to Arizona.

John Ringo and his three companions had ridden down to Animas Valley, past the dead and silent ranches of Curly Bill and Old Man Clanton, on through San Luis Pass into Mexico. There they turned west, followed out the Rio de Carretas until they came to a settlement.

"Ought to be shying clear of these towns," Ike Clanton said, remembering the fate that had befallen his father. "Some of these Mexicans are liable to recognize us."

Ringo shook his head. "We never raided this far down. Anyway, we have to eat."

"And I'm dead broke," Swilling said. "Got to figure a way to get my hands on some cash."

"One thing you won't find very plentiful around here," Pony Deal said. "Maybe we'd be better off to keep riding until we hit one of the big towns."

Ringo said, "All right with me. You pick it. All these burgs look alike far as I'm concerned."

"Don't make no difference to you just so's there's a saloon handy, that it?" Ike Clanton remarked, cocking his head to one side.

Ringo favored him with a cool look. "Any time my drinking bothers you, Ike—move on."

"Didn't say it bothered me, did I? Always wondered though why it didn't slow you down some, like it does the rest of us. Doesn't seem to have much effect on you."

Ringo made no reply, simply rode on in complete silence. Clanton said, "Man usually drinks liquor because it fires him up aplenty, makes him feel good. Seems you got some other reason, Johnny. What is it?"

"My own," Ringo said bluntly. "Man can find a lot of good company inside a bottle if he looks for it. And it's usually better than what he comes up against outside."

They pushed on, always bearing west. They robbed a store in a small settlement that night, got little money but were able to lay in a supply of food for the trail.

"Got a friend in a place called Fronteras," Pony Deal said when they resumed the march the next morning. "Be a good place to lay up."

"How far from here?" Swilling asked.

"Thirty, forty miles."

Clanton turned to Deal. "You ain't figuring to go back to Tombstone?"

"Sure, once things blow over. Hate to spend the rest of my life in this Godforsaken country."

"Way I feel, too. I figure if we go back, we can get things going again. Call the boys together and pick up right where we broke off—"

"You still chewin' on that old rag? What about Earp?"

"He'll simmer down."

Swilling wasn't so certain. "Maybe about some things, but not when it comes to Morgan and Virgil. He's blaming us for killing Morg and crippling Virgil. He ain't likely to get over that."

"Then," Clanton said boldly, "expect our first job will be to get rid of Wyatt. I ain't forgetting what he done to Billy and the McLowrys."

Ringo glanced at Clanton, gave him a slow, dry smile. "Seems I remember you had a few chances to get even with Wyatt, only you never took advantage of any of them."

Ike stirred uncomfortably. "Don't you worry, I'll hold up my end of the bargain when the times comes."

Swilling laughed. "Like you done at the O.K. Corral?"

Clanton swore, his face bright red. "Damn it! You keep talking about that! Things weren't right that day. I didn't get half a chance."

Pony Deal, aware of the slow rise of anger among the three men, said, "Well, maybe you'll get a second try when we go back."

"Not at Wyatt," Ringo said quietly. "He's my chore. I owe him for Curly Bill."

They reached Fronteras the next day. Deal located his friend, a man he called Candido, and they set up quarters in an adobe shack at the rear of his cantina, or saloon.

The dry, blistering-hot days melted one into another in an endless monotony and finally the restlessness began to grow within John Ringo, as it did also with the others. There was talk of going deeper into Mexico, of swinging back up to Texas, of going to Kansas. There was a woman in Santa Fe Swilling would like to see again. And then one evening Pony Deal shattered the sameness with some startling news.

"Johnny, you recall that tinhorn gambler you and some of the boys nearly lynched in Charleston? The one they called Johnny-Behind-the-Deuce?"

"Sure do," Ringo said. "Chased him all the way to Tombstone, and Wyatt and a bunch of deputies saved his neck for him and took him to Tucson. Heard later he broke jail and was down here in Mexico somewhere."

"He is—or was. Ran into him this afternoon. Was heading back for Tombstone. Says the Earps have skipped the country. Last he heard of Wyatt, he was somewhere in Colorado."

"By God!" Ike Clanton said in a thankful voice. "Now we can get out of this place."

"Means Earp and his federal deputies have quit," Ringo said, thinking aloud. "The tinhorn say what Wyatt was doing in Colorado?"

"He didn't know. Expect he got tired of Tombstone when things quieted down. But he'll be coming back. He's a big man in Cochise County now."

"Probably right. Where's Swilling? He know about this?"

"Was with me when I talked to the tinhorn. He'll be along pretty soon."

"I'm getting my gear together right now," Ike Clanton said, rising. "Sooner I shake the dust of this dump off my boots, better I'll like it."

Candido, his long, swarthy face solemn, appeared in the doorway at that moment. He motioned to Pony Deal, who got to his feet and walked out into the yard. He and the Mexican talked for several minutes and then the little gunman returned.

"Won't have to wait on Swilling," he said.

Ringo glanced up. "Why? What's happened to him?"

"Tried to hold up a cantina at the other end of town. They shot him down. He's dead."

Ringo's face hardened. "Know who did it?"

"No. Half a dozen in on it, Candido says. Nobody knows just who they are. Way it generally turns out around here when a gringo gets killed. Nobody ever knows anything."

Ike Clanton continued to stuff his belongings into his saddlebags. "Tough on Hank. Reckon he was trying to get himself a little stake together before we headed back to Tombstone."

Ringo stared at the floor. "Ought to square things for him before we pull out, but we can't take on the whole town."

"Right," Pony Deal said. "About all we can do is forget it."

23

They rode into Tombstone three abreast, boldly and with no show of fear. They traveled the length of Allen Street, passing the Bird Cage Theatre, where a road show was unloading scenery for the evening performance; the Wells Fargo office, where three men stood in the doorway and watched in frowning silence; on by the Oriental, the Crystal Palace, Vogan's Bowling Alley, where Johnny-Behind-the-Deuce had been hidden, the hotels, Hafford's Saloon, and finally they halted at the corral on the corner of Third Street.

They dismounted, turned their worn horses over to the hostler, and started back up the dusty avenue, walking an arm's length apart in that careful way of men not sure what the succeeding moments might hold but ready for any eventuality.

"Looks the same," Pony Deal murmured. "Same old buildings, same signs. Same people, mostly."

"Place won't change much in a couple of months," Ike Clanton said.

But John Ringo was noticing a difference. The street was the same, yes; the dry, hot air, the loose, grayish dust, the sounds and smells were as before. Yet there was change. He saw it in the expressions of men who watched with close, narrow interest; in the eyes of those who feared to be anything but outwardly friendly. The Curly Bills, the Hank Swillings, the Pete Spences were gone, and for all time thereafter.

"I'd say we're alone here," he muttered. "The last of the old bunch."

"Bound to be some of the boys around," Ike Clanton protested. "Just got to be. Know damn well Phin's still alive and kicking."

"There's Billy Claiborne!" Deal said suddenly. "Over there in front of Hafford's."

"Good," Ringo said. "Let's have a drink with him and find out a few things."

They swung off to the left, angled toward the saloon. Claiborne came off the porch, his face wreathed in a broad smile.

"Johnny! Pony! Ike! Sure good to see you back! Where you been keeping yourselves?"

"South," Clanton said, as they paused to shake hands. "You the only one around? Where is everybody?"

Claiborne shook his head. "Reckon I'm about it. See Phin once in a while. You're the first of the crowd to show up."

"Where's Phin now?" Ike wondered.

"Probably out at your place on the San Pedro. Come on inside. Let's have a drink for old times."

"Old times," Pony Deal echoed. "Reckon that's about all

we can do for the old days—have a drink."

They entered the saloon, settled at a table in a back corner. A few men turned to them as they crossed the room, some smiling, others strained and vaguely hostile. The figure of Buckskin Frank Leslie, wearing the fringed leather coat that had given him his name, detached itself from the bar and moved toward them. Smiling, he offered his hand all around.

"Good to see you boys again," he said. "Mind if I sit down?"

Ringo said, "Help yourself."

The bartender brought a bottle and glasses, deposited them on the table, and wheeled away. He was a stranger.

Ike Clanton poured drinks for all. "Things look plenty quiet around here," he said, leaning back in his chair.

Leslie said, "They damn sure are! Some of the mines flooded out and shut down. There's a strike or two going on and silver's not worth what it was. Outside that, the town's in good shape."

"Behan still the sheriff?"

Claiborne nodded. "Yeah, but he's got himself a whole hatful of trouble. After Earp got turned loose in Denver, a grand jury got on Behan's back. Indicted him over a big mess of things. He's hopping around like a three-legged jack rabbit trying to get squared away."

"Doubt if he'll be overjoyed at seeing you three," Leslie drawled.

"From the looks on the faces of a few citizens on the street, I don't think many were," Pony Deal said with a short laugh.

"If you don't mind my asking, what brought you back?"

Leslie asked in a casual voice.

"Sort of figured to get some of the boys together, start an outfit of my—our own," Clanton said. "Could headquarter out at my place on the San Pedro, or maybe the old man's ranch on the Animas."

"Sounds good!" Billy Claiborne exclaimed. "Sure could use some cash."

"Wouldn't be worth the trouble," Leslie said, refilling his glass. "Hardly any shipments of bullion going out any more. Fact is, they'd about stopped before you left, only things were happening so fast nobody noticed it."

"Always cattle," Pony Deal said.

"That's changed, too. Ranchers around here are plenty tough now. They'll string a man up if he just looks sideways at a cow or horse. Guess they figure they're not going to ever let things get like they were a year or two ago. Anybody pulls one raid, the whole county takes up the hunt."

Deal shifted his gaze to Ringo. The tall outlaw was slumped in his chair, face solemn, eyes deep and remote. "Looks like you were right, Johnny."

"Town dies out, gets old, same as a man," Ringo said.

Ike Clanton shook his head stubbornly. "Well, I ain't believing things are so tough."

Leslie looked at him thoughtfully. "Way it goes. Some have to learn things the hard way."

Clanton said, "That's me—right down the line. Well, think I'll ride over to Charleston—"

"Turning into a ghost town—"

". . . And look up Phin. You boys decide you want to get things started, come on out to the ranch and we'll jaw about it."

Clanton pushed back his chair, the legs screeching noisily on the bare floor. He spun on his heel and started for the door. Someone standing at the end of the bar said something to him as he passed. He grinned, nodded, and went on.

"Ike's a fool," Ringo murmured. "He thinks things are just the same as they were around here before. You still at the Oriental, Frank?"

"Not regular," Leslie replied. "Owners of the saloons are doing their own bartending, mostly. Get along without hired hands, way business is."

"And with the Earps gone, you've got nobody to work on the side for."

Leslie's eyes narrowed. He looked more closely at Ringo. "Sometimes a man has to pick up a little extra change where he can find it."

"Sure, sure. And Wyatt paid a man pretty good to ride in his posses. But forget it. I have. How's gambling? Can a man keep himself going at the tables?"

Buckskin Frank nodded. "One thing that's still going good. Only change is there's no real big money floating around any more."

"Man never needs much," Ringo said. "Enough to buy whiskey, a bed, and a bite to eat now and then."

Billy Claiborne frowned, his face mirroring disappointment. "You don't figure on getting the boys together again?"

Ringo shook his head. "Not up to me. Let Ike try if he wants to."

"You sure wouldn't be bothered by Earp," Leslie said.

Ringo lifted his cold glance to the gambler. "What

about Wyatt?"

Leslie said, "Nothing much. He's not around, that's all. Never came back from Colorado. Guess nobody knows exactly where he is."

John Clum, one-time mayor of Tombstone and fire-tongued editor of the *Epitaph*, pushed through the doors and halted at the bar. He gave the four men at the table sharp appraisal, tossed off his shot of liquor, and departed.

"Reckon he's got some news to print now," Pony Deal said, and grinned.

"Not him," Leslie replied. "Don't own the newspaper any more. Sold out."

"That sure ought to have made Behan happy. Didn't any of the Earps ever come back?"

Leslie said, "None of them. Not likely to, either. Especially Wyatt. He made too many enemies—and the friends he's got who'd back him up now aren't the shooting kind. Johnny, you feel like setting in a few hands of poker?"

Ringo said, "Fine. There a game going somewhere?"

"Plenty of penny-ante stuff, sure; but we could get a good one going over in my cabin. Might be a good idea for you and Pony to keep out of sight a couple of days, anyway—until the surprise of your coming back wears off. I expect you'll be having visitors. The vigilante committee is going to want to know your plans. Behan will be wanting to know, too."

"Can give them the answer right now," Ringo said. "I'm going to set myself down to a lot of serious drinking and card playing. Outside that, I've got no plans."

The four men arose, left the saloon. They crossed Allen Street, walked uninterrupted down Fourth and turned onto

Toughnut, where Leslie was at the moment living. They entered his small house, went to a back room, where a table and half a dozen chairs were already set up.

They played steadily until near midnight, with Ringo and Leslie taking most of the money. Two more players came into the game and a fresh supply of liquor was brought in. Shortly after three o'clock Pony Deal went broke and dropped out. He hung around until the first streaks of daylight began to show in the east, and then started for the door.

"You want me, Johnny, I'll be at the Clanton place," he said, and left.

The game continued, with each player stopping periodically, and then only briefly, for a few minutes' sleep, or to stretch and get a breath of air outside the smoke-filled room. The two newcomers lost their stakes, quit, were replaced by three others. Word of the game had gotten around and now there were spectators.

Ringo drank steadily, played on in his deadly, silent manner. The day passed. Lights came on again in Tombstone. Ten o'clock . . . midnight . . . Billy Claiborne was showing the signs of wear. At four in the morning Frank Leslie pushed back his chair. Ringo was heavy winner.

"Had enough," the gambler said, pulling on his fringed coat. "What I'd like is a ride across the hills, get my head cleared up." His voice was thick and his sagging face and slightly glazed eyes reflected the effects of the whiskey and long physical inactivity.

Claiborne said, "I'll sure quit if the rest are willing."

All voiced their agreement, with the exception of John Ringo. He pulled himself out of his slouch, slowly raked in the coins and currency that lay before him on the table. Methodically he picked up his winnings, stuffed them into his pockets.

"No players, no game," he said philosophically. He got to his feet, swung his attention to Buckskin Frank. "Let's all just take that ride—you and Billy and me. Couple of old places I'd like to visit."

24

They took the road southeast toward Antelope Springs. At McCann's new place, some ten miles out from Tombstone, they halted, dismounted, and went inside to escape the steadily rising heat.

For a time they sat around and mixed their conversation concerning the old days with liberal quantities of whiskey and then, one by one, fell asleep. They awoke later, began a new poker game and drinking bout that ran for the better part of the next two days and nights.

This broke up finally, to McCann's relief, as Ringo and Leslie were continually quarreling over incidentals, and they rode off. They paused at Soldier's Holes, a locality not far from the old McLowry ranch in Sulphur Springs Valley. From there they drifted on to a saloon in Myers Cienega and repeated the McCann's performance.

Early the next morning Ringo, in bad shape, pulled off alone, an urge to see Galeyville possessing him. He did not awaken Leslie or Billy Claiborne, but rode quietly off into the cool Arizona daylight. Some distance later he came abreast of a rancher, who spoke as he passed, but Ringo glanced at him through hazy, unseeing eyes and continued on.

As the hours moved by and he rode on through the blasting heat of midday, the whiskey in his body lashed at him mercilessly. Somehow he stayed on his horse and near dark, in the foothills of the Chiricahuas, he halted. He remained for a time on the saddle, slumped forward, and then finally he fell and lay prone on the ground.

The coolness of the night eventually brought him to semi-consciousness. He roused, and moving to his horse, dug the last bottle of whiskey from the saddlebags. There was only a little left in it and he turned it to his parched lips and drank it all without pausing.

He settled back on the sandy earth, fell asleep quickly under the drugging influence of the liquor. Near midnight he again awakened, stared about. He had intended to reach Galeyville long before that hour—and here he was still on the wrong side of the mountains. He found his horse grazing nearby and climbed onto the animal with difficulty. His eyes were swollen almost shut and his mind, punished by many days and nights of steady drinking, little food and sleep, functioned indifferently.

He put the horse into motion, pointed him eastward, and gave him his head. He pushed on through the night, half conscious, and when daylight finally broke, he came to and was surprised and angered to discover he was still in the Sulphur Springs Valley. The horse had taken the wrong turn at some time during the night hours. Ringo again halted, dismounted, cursing the animal unreasonably for something that was no real fault of its own.

But the weary brute was no nearer total exhaustion than John Ringo himself. Ringo needed sleep and a chance to let the overpowering effects of the whiskey wear off. He glanced about. A broadly spreading oak tree with a fan of deep shade offered an inviting place in which to rest. He removed his coat and boots, hung them on the saddle. Picketing the horse in a small clump of brush, he started to climb the short embankment to the tree. Sharp burs and rocks dug into his feet. He took an old undershirt from his saddlebags, ripped it apart and wrapped them, improvising a means for protection.

Even in his befuddled state the old instincts did not forsake John Ringo. He pulled his rifle from its scabbard, touched the ivory-handled pistol at his hip to assure himself of its presence. He climbed then to the shadows beneath the oak. He propped the carbine against the tree's trunk and settled back. A long sigh slipped from his lips. He would rest for a little while. After that he would ride on to Galeyville. He was asleep immediately. . . .

EPILOGUE

Ringo—the deadliest gunman of them all!

John Yoast, recovering from his initial shock, summoned several neighbors and assembled a coroner's jury. Death was a frequent incident in and around Tombstone and likely there were few men living in Cochise County who had never been called upon to serve on such a panel. The procedures were familiar to all.

They viewed the body, examined the effects. All agreed that it was John Ringo. A bullet had entered the head at the right temple, passed out through the top of the head, doing terrible damage in its brutal flight. Someone remarked that a part of the scalp was missing, that it appeared as though it had been cut off with a knife.

There were no other marks of violence on the body and this was duly noted. Ringo was dressed in hat, shirt, vest, pants, and drawers. His feet were clad in socks and further protected, for some reason, by strips of cloth that looked like an undershirt. He had not walked any distance. His revolver was in his hand. It had not been fired and contained five cartridges, with the hammer of the pistol resting on the empty sixth cylinder chamber. This was a customary procedure for men who knew and carried such a weapon.

His rifle was nearby, leaning against the tree. It, also, had not been discharged. A live shell was in the chamber and ten more waited in the magazine. Two cartridge belts were around his waist, one containing bullets for the pistol, the other for the rifle. That was all of it. They recorded the date—July 14, 1882.

The verdict John Yoast and his jury reached was startling: suicide.

They buried John Ringo where they had found him, piling a high mound of rocks upon the grave. While this was being done, his horse was found and additional information concerning it—the boots and coat tied to the saddle, the empty whiskey bottle, the condition of the animal—was added to the account. Then all rode into Tombstone and reported their findings to the official coroner. He considered the verdict, disagreed immediately, but since he had not and could not see the body personally, he filed a certificate which said, simply: ". . . cause of death unknown, but supposed gunshot wound."

Rumors spread through Tombstone like a wind-whipped brush fire. Some, including the new editor of the *Epitaph*, concurred with the suicide theory. They ascribed such action to Ringo's usual dark frame of mind, the quantity of liquor he had consumed in the past week or ten days, the demise of the outlaw gang and the men he had ridden with, and a dozen other reasons.

None of these stood close scrutiny. Charges and suspicions began to run wild. Bill Saunders, the rancher who had seen Ringo riding away from Myers Cienega that morning, recalled that a short time later he had come upon Buckskin Frank Leslie. Leslie had asked him if he had seen anything of Ringo, and Saunders had replied he had passed the man earlier, that he was farther up the trail. Leslie had ridden on in pursuit.

Immediately there were those who concluded Leslie to be the killer. But Billy Claiborne had also been one of Ringo's last drinking partners. He, too, had been at Myers Cienega. He quickly became another suspect.

And there was Wyatt Earp. Some believed the lawman had returned; that he had come upon the sleeping Ringo, further incapacitated by liquor, and exacted his vengeance for deeds past and hate still present. But such was scarcely in keeping with Earp's character, and no one had actually seen him in Cochise County since he had ridden north to Colorado. Few believed it was Earp.

Yet John Ringo was dead—and buried. Suicide? Hardly.

No man, even so peerless a gunhawk as he, could have held a pistol to his own temple, blasted away the top of his head, then removed and replaced the empty shell casing in the cylinder; nor could he have fired the rifle, ejected by lever the spent cartridge, and stood the weapon against the tree. It could not be possible—not in the wildest reaches of fantastic imagination, or in the cold, sober consideration of a man's reflex actions.

Pony Deal probably had the answer. He remembered Johnny-Behind-the-Deuce. He recalled the incident at Charleston, the near lynching, the burning hatred for Ringo that never died in the gambler's heart. He remembered, too, the tinhorn's return to Arizona and Tombstone only a short time prior to their own; he drew his own conclusions: Johnny-Behind-the-Deuce had come upon Ringo sleeping off his prolonged drunk. It was the opportunity he had hoped for. He seized it, put a bullet through the head of his old enemy.

Pony Deal, as befit the code, hunted up Johnny-Behind-the-Deuce and killed him. He then went on to meet his own death a short time later in a gunfight near the town of Clifton.

Billy Claiborne pinned the onus on Buckskin Frank Leslie. In November of 1882 he rode into Tombstone declaring volubly that he was back for one purpose only—to kill the man who had murdered his friend John Ringo. That man, he said, was Leslie. Claiborne's friends endeavored to calm him, knowing that compared to the gambler, Billy was a rank greenhorn when it came to handling a gun.

Claiborne brushed them all aside, called Buckskin Frank into the street for a showdown, and was promptly killed.

Leslie was brought to account for the shooting and cleared. He had been given no choice except to defend himself and his honor. But the stain remained and there were those at Billy Claiborne's side when he drew his last breaths who claimed to have heard him say: "Frank Leslie murdered John Ringo. I helped carry Ringo there and seen him do it."

And many people believed that, for they say dying men do not lie but gush forth the absolute truth in hopes of ensuring a better hereafter for themselves.

Billy Claiborne was the last. Shortly before that final, flaming incident, Ike Clanton, still determined to revive the old days, had been caught rustling cattle. With him were his brother, Phin, and two or three raw recruits to the game. What happened to the fledglings is not clear but Ike died in a hail of bullets from the enraged rancher's rifle, and Phin was captured and sentenced to a term in Yuma prison.

All such was mere afterglow. It could be said that tall, brooding John Ringo and lawless, lusty, turbulent, and rich Tombstone died together.

ACKNOWLEDGMENTS

To the following authors and their books, which were invaluable in cross-checking reports, incidents, and dates, grateful acknowledgment is herewith made. Also, to the individuals, establishments, libraries, and historical repositories who so graciously opened to me or examined their files and gave of their time and effort, I am indebted and extend my appreciation.

Bartholomew, Ed. *Biographical Album of Western Gunfighters.* Ruidoso, New Mexico: Frontier Book Company, 1958.

Breakenridge, William. *Helldorado.* Boston: Houghton Mifflin Company, 1927.

Burns, Walter Noble. *Tombstone.* New York: Doubleday, Doran & Company, Inc., 1927.

Chisholm, Joseph. *Brewery Gulch.* San Antonio, Texas: The Naylor Company, 1949.

Croy, Homer. *Last of the Great Outlaws.* New York: Duell, Sloan and Pearce, 1956.

Lake, Stuart N. *Wyatt Earp, Frontier Marshal.* Boston: Houghton Mifflin Company, 1931.

Martin, Douglas D. (ed.). *Tombstone's Epitaph.* Albuquerque, New Mexico: University of New Mexico Press, 1957.

Myers, John Myers, *The Tombstone Story.* New York: Grosset & Dunlap, Inc., 1951.

Sonnichsen, C. L. *Ten Texas Feuds.* Albuquerque, New Mexico: University of New Mexico Press, 1957.

Walters, L. D. *Tombstone's Yesterday.* Tucson, Arizona: Acme Printing Company, 1928.
Waters, William. *Gallery of Western Bad Men.* Covington, Kentucky: Americana Publications, 1954.
Filed copies of the newspapers *Tombstone Epitaph* and *Tombstone Nugget.*

Miss Margaret Bierschwale, Mason, Texas. John Myers Myers, Tempe, Arizona. Chamber of Commerce, San Jose, California. James M. Day, Texas State Library, Austin, Texas. R. S. Weddle, *The Menard News*, Menard, Texas. Fernando Pesqueira, Biblioteca y Museo de Donora, Hermosillo, Sonora, Mexico. J. R. K. Kantor, The Bancroft Library, University of California, Berkeley, California. Maryland Historical Society, Baltimore, Maryland. Aaron Spelling, Four Star Television, Hollywood, California. Clyde Arbuckle, Historic Landmarks Commission, City of San Jose, California. Wayne E. Wade, Oak Hill Memorial Park and Mortuary, San Jose, California. Board of Supervisors, County of Cochise, Bisbee, Arizona. Donald Younger, Santa Cruz, California.

Public libraries in Albuquerque, New Mexico; Phoenix, Arizona; El Paso, Texas; Tombstone, Arizona, and elsewhere.

Center Point Publishing
600 Brooks Road • P.O Box 1
Thorndike ME 04986-0001 USA

(207) 568-3717

US & Canada:
1 800 929-9108